We sat in the same U configuration, in every class. All twenty of us. The Espies. Together. All friggin' day.

The school didn't want us mixing with the rest of the senior class. Which was ridiculous. We had ESP, not Ebola. A curriculum had been tailored just for us, to help us prepare for what lay ahead. Not that anyone knew what lay ahead. It's not like there had ever been an entire class of telepaths before.

Yup. We had telepathy. We read minds. We got it two years ago from our flu shots. Twenty-two sophomores from homeroom 10B, plus one freshman and one senior, all from the same contaminated batch.

The future awaited us and was ours to command. ESP was our magic wand.

Or so we thought.

It turns out, magic wands can break.

THINK TWICE

Sarah Mlynowski

ORCHARD

ORCHARD BOOKS

First published in Great Britain in 2016 by The Watts Publishing Group

1 3 5 7 9 10 8 6 4 2

Text © Sarah Mlynowski, 2016

The moral rights of the author have been asserted.

A CIP catalogue record for this book is available from the British Library.

ISBN 978 1 40833 155 2

Printed and bound in Great Britain by CPI Group (UK) Ltd, Croydon, CR0 4YY

The paper and board used in this book are made from wood from responsible sources.

Orchard Books
An imprint of Hachette Children's Group
Part of The Watts Publishing Group Limited
Carmelite House
50 Victoria Embankment
London EC4Y 0DZ

An Hachette UK Company
www.hachette.co.uk

www.hachettechildrens.co.uk

For Elissa Ambrose. Mom and mind reader.

To: <u>StoddardLawrence@usa.cia.gov</u>
Date: November 1st
From: <u>DailSuzanna@usa.cia.gov</u>
Subject: Recruitment

Dear Lawrence,

Below, please find my assessment of the twenty remaining Espies.

As you know, I've been monitoring them for the past two and a half years, since they were sophomores and first became telepathic from their flu shots. I hope you find my report satisfactory and that it aids the selection process for Operation Diamond.

ESPIES, ROOM 12B, BLOOMBERG HIGH SCHOOL

1. Barak, Michelle
One of the few Espies not living in Tribeca. She lives in a fourth-floor walkup in Midtown. Obsessed with romance novels, particularly ones about princesses and princes.
Not recommended: Spends too much time reading and is mostly sedentary.

2. Bhatt, Mona
The only Espie junior. Dating Espie #13, George Marson. She was one of the ones who we discovered later in the year.
Not recommended: Still has another year of high school.

3. Brohman-Maizner, Jordana

Overly concerned with her physical appearance, e.g. walks around with a full manicure set, multiple lipsticks. Wears hair extensions, false eyelashes, and would like breast implants. Values fame to an unhealthy degree. Agreed to appear in that horrible reality show about their ESP, *We Know What You're Thinking*.

Not recommended: Displays reduced mental capacity.

4. Byrne, Olivia

Aspires to be a doctor. Dating Espie #15, Cooper Miller.

Not recommended: She once had severe anxiety – could potentially resurface if faced with extreme stress.

5. Cole, Brian James (familiarly known as BJ)

Discusses sex and sexuality constantly. Dating Espie #6, Tess Demir.

Not recommended: National security is far from his mind.

6. Demir, Tess

Talented writer. Dating Espie #5, Brian James Cole.

Not recommended: Has a need to be open and truthful.

7. Feldman, Mackenzie

Despite having the most talent in the class, and being extremely attractive (could be used as a honeypot to seduce targets?), she is not a motivated student and might not have the necessary confidence to be successful.

Not recommended: Too risky.

8. Ferrero, Brinn
Weird, weird, weird. Loves fencing and strange clothing. Mumbles.
Not recommended: Too weird.

9. Gaw, Nick
Star baseball player. Already being recruited by top athletic
programs.
Not recommended: He's a bit of a pothead. And he would never
agree to give up baseball. Also, his mother is a teacher here at
Bloomberg High and would likely kill me if he was recruited.

10. Hunter, Courtney
Self-centered. She also stars in *We Know What You're Thinking*.
Not recommended: Craves fame.

11. Jenkins, Levi
Surrounds himself with Espie groupies.
Not recommended: Craves attention.

12. Kolar, Anojah
Nice girl. Excellent morals. Refuses to wear her glasses since it
seems to increase the volume of her ESP.
Not recommended: Perfect eyesight is obviously preferred in this
program.

13. Marson, George (familiarly known as Mars)
Piano prodigy. Dating Espie #2, Mona Bhatt.
Not recommended: Too artistic – i.e., too emotional.

14. McMann, Edward

Likes anything related to the paranormal, especially vampires.
Dresses in all black.
Not recommended: Creepy.

15. Miller, Cooper

Pothead, gambler. Dating Espie #4, Olivia Byrne.
Not recommended: Does not take anything seriously.

16. Newman, Sadie

Mature for her age; likes to date older men.
Not recommended: Falls in love too easily, would be distracted.

17. Philips, Isaac

Nice guy. Secure in his sexual orientation.
Not recommended: His refusal to dye his hair – he's entirely gray!
– illustrates his desire to stand out, as opposed to blend in.

18. Ricci, Polly (familiarly known as Pi)

Smart, ambitious, focused.
***Recommended: Shows strong leadership ability. Would have no
moral qualms or hesitations about "taking care" of any "problem".

19. Zacow, Daniel (identical twin brother of David Zacow, Espie #20)

Aspires to perform in Las Vegas.
Not recommended: Too flaky.

20. Zacow, David (identical twin brother of Daniel Zacow, Espie #19)
Aspires to perform in Las Vegas.
Not recommended: Too flaky.

As you can see, the only candidate I can recommend is Polly Ricci, Espie #18, for her exceptional mental capacity and relentless ambition. She would be an asset to your "special team".

As a personal note, I'll be pleased when this is over. Teaching Lab to telepaths at a Manhattan high school is not my ideal undercover placement. There was a reason I didn't have children. Teenagers smell like feet.

Sincerely,

Dr Suzanna Dail
CIA Operative

Chapter One
HELLO, AGAIN

Cooper Miller, in jeans and a wrinkled black T-shirt, walked into the classroom singing, "Happy April Fool's Day to us. Happy April Fool's Day to us. Happy April Fool's Day to uuuuuuus..."

Polly Ricci, aka Pi, the class brainiac, straightened her shoulders. *Does he have to sing all the time? It's so annoying.*

Cooper barely missed a beat. "Happy April Fool's Day to us. Happy April Fool's Day to us. Happy April Fool's Day to uuuuuuss..."

He took his seat in the back next to Nick Gaw, his best friend since preschool. Nick was asleep, his head down on his desk. Baseball training had started the week before, and Nick was wiped. All the pot he smoked with Cooper didn't help.

Cooper smiled at his girlfriend and sat down.

One look at him, and Olivia was thinking about how cute he was. Soft blue eyes. Delicious lips. She was crazy about him.

Delicious lips? Really?

What do they taste like? Chocolate?

Mmm. Chocolate.

Olivia and Cooper sitting in a tree! K-I-S-S-I-N-G!

Olivia's cheeks heated up and she closed her eyes.

Closing our eyes blocked transmission.

In walked Mackenzie Feldman, Cooper's ex-girlfriend, in skinny jeans and an off-the-shoulder shirt. It wasn't meant to be off-the-shoulder, but the neck was too tight, so she'd given it a trim. It looked funky, so she wore it.

We all thought it looked pretty good. But she looked good in everything.

She heard the thoughts about Cooper and Olivia, but they only mildly annoyed her. She and Cooper broke up sophomore year. He could date whoever he wanted. What did she care? She glanced at him as he prodded Nick awake, but then he caught her eye and she looked away.

Mackenzie took her seat in the row across from the window, next to Tess Demir. Tess was Mackenzie's best friend. Tess's boyfriend, Brian Joseph Cole, sat on her other side. Levi Jenkins was next to BJ.

Our desks were arranged in a horseshoe. That way, the tall people didn't block the short ones. We didn't have to look directly at someone to hear his thoughts, but there couldn't be someone in the way. That's why the horseshoe worked. No one was blocked. The teacher's desk was at the top of the room, while ours faced toward the center, where our thoughts pooled.

We sat in the same U configuration, in every class. All twenty of us. The Espies. Together. All friggin' day.

The school didn't want us mixing with the rest of the senior class. Which was ridiculous. We had ESP, not Ebola. A curriculum had been tailored just for us, to help us prepare for what lay ahead. Not that anyone knew what lay ahead. It's not like there had ever been an entire class of telepaths before.

Yup. We had telepathy. We read minds. We got it two years ago from our flu shots. Twenty-two sophomores from homeroom 10B, plus one freshman and one senior, all from the same contaminated batch.

At least none of us got the flu.

Hardy har har.

"Good morning, my bright and shining telepaths," Mr Jonas said, closing the door. He looked around the room. "I see Mars is absent. Mona, too."

Are they sick?

I heard mono's going around. Some of the freshmen have it.

Are you kidding me? If Mars and Mona give the rest of us mono, I'll kill them.

Have you kissed either of them lately?

No!

How did they get mono?

Mars's sister's a freshman.

He made out with his sister?

We laughed.

"What's so funny?" Mr Jonas asked, sitting down at his desk. No one replied.

"C'mon, someone has to tell me. It's only fair." He adjusted the sunglasses on his nose. Unlike us, our teachers did not have telepathy. Hence the glasses. Sunglasses, like closing your eyes, blocked transmission. At first we thought it was because of the tint: the darker, the better. Which meant people were constantly walking into walls. But it was the polarization. It filtered out thoughts along with the glare. Originally we wore glasses all the time. But by mid-junior year we had decided it was everyone else's problem, not ours.

Mr Jonas cleared his throat. "Fine, then. I know today's a big day for seniors. Is anyone here still waiting to hear about college acceptances?"

We all shook our heads. Some of us laughed.

Is he kidding?

Didn't we all get in months ago?

Yes. Of course we did.

True, not every school wanted us on their campus – *Screw you, Yale* – but a lot of them did. It wasn't just that the psych departments were hoping to get us in their labs. We were C-list celebrities, like a child actor or a governor's kid. Except we had actual abilities, amazing abilities, and the entire world knew it.

In the beginning, back when we were sophomores, we tried not to tell anyone.

But then all our parents had found out in a crazy meeting with the Food and Drug Administration. Most of them had been in shock. They couldn't wrap their heads around it. It was hard to wrap *our* heads around it. Then we decided not to take the antidote and a lot of the parents were furious. Some were just nervous. No one wanted kids who could hear their every thought.

The FDA had asked us to keep our skills a secret. But secrets were hard to keep. Especially this secret, since it involved twenty-four teenagers plus forty-seven parents plus ten stepparents. Some of us told siblings. And then best friends. And then girlfriends and boyfriends and then and then and then…

Obviously, we knew when other people knew. No one could keep a secret from us.

At first, we denied it. We didn't want to be freaks. But then a random senior told her mom, who happened to be an editor at *The New York Post*. When the article about us came out, our lives pretty much exploded.

The reporters camped out at the school that entire first year. They talked about us on *TMZ*. They talked about us on *60 Minutes*. Some of us, like Courtney and Jordana, liked the fame. Some of us, like Pi and Olivia, wanted nothing to do with it. The media hadn't been allowed to list our names or show our photos without permission since we were minors, so those of us who chose to be were kept out of the public eye.

The next year there were fewer reporters, but a lot more gawkers. And tons of offers, especially for TV commercials that went along the lines of: "Oh, no! I can hear him thinking about my bad breath! I wish I had Quadruplemint Gum!" Most of us declined. We didn't need the money, or the notoriety. Courtney and Jordana did a few of the spots, but stopped when they started their reality show. Last year they filmed in New York. This season the plan was to fly them to different locations. The theme was Telepaths Take America.

Anyway. This year, those of us who had applied to colleges had all been quick to milk our ESP experiences for our personal essays.

What else was I going to write about? BJ thought now, leaning back in his chair. *My sex life?*

What sex life? Levi thought.

Even though they'd been together for two and a half years, BJ and Tess had never done it.

We knew they hadn't because it was all BJ could think about: *if* they were going to do it, *when* they were going to do it, *why* they hadn't already done it.

Tess wanted to have sex, she just didn't want all the Espies to have front row seats.

Tess glared across the horseshoe at Levi. *Not everyone enjoys meaningless sex with groupies.*

Levi loved the groupies. The rest of us thought they were pathetic. Once we came out to the world, some people wanted nothing to do with us, but others wanted to be around us all the time. It wasn't the fame they craved; they wanted to be understood. It was like going to a shrink without paying.

Next year, Levi was going to the University of Miami. Hello, groupies in bikinis.

Tess and BJ were both going to Berkeley.

Mars was going to Julliard.

Cooper had only applied to NYU, and had gotten in. He

wasn't sure what he wanted to study. Could he study video games? He liked playing video games. He also liked playing poker. He'd picked it up when he'd been hanging out at his mom's house in Jersey over the summer. There was a group of guys he played with a few times a week.

They did not know about his extra talent. He told them his name was Leo.

Olivia had gotten into NYU, Brown and Johns Hopkins. NYU and Brown had offered her full scholarships, but she was still waiting to hear if Johns Hopkins would too. They had her dream pre-med program, but unlike the majority of us Espies, she couldn't afford the tuition.

Mackenzie had gotten into Stanford, just like her brother and sister, even though her grades were crap. She'd applied to prove to her siblings that she could get in too, now that she had ESP. Once she'd gotten in, she felt like she had to go. Her siblings were convinced she would flunk out. She was pretty sure she would, too.

Not everyone was going to college. Some of us were taking different roads. Courtney and Jordana, legends in their own minds, wanted to continue their career in reality TV. The first season of their show hadn't been as big of a hit as they'd hoped, but it got renewed, so maybe it wasn't that terrible. Inane, definitely. We'd all watched the first few episodes, but we'd had to stop. Did we care about what random people were thinking? Did we care that half the men on the show were cheating on their wives, or that half the women had Botox/boob jobs/tummy tucks? No, we did not.

Dave and Daniel, the twins, had also been offered a TV show, but were working on a telepathy act instead. As soon as school was done, they were planning on moving to Vegas. We weren't too sure about that. It seemed unlikely that the casinos would let anyone with ESP within ten feet of their tables.

Pi had been offered a job as a spy. Yes, a spy. She had also been accepted to Harvard.

With the exception of Mona, who was a junior, we were all making plans for next year, post-high school.

The future awaited us and was ours to command. ESP was our magic wand.

Or so we thought.

It turns out, magic wands can break.

Mr Jonas stepped into the center of our horseshoe. "Let's get started."

Chapter Two
BURSTING BUBBLES

Olivia couldn't have been happier.

"What?" Cooper asked.

Olivia blushed. "Nothing."

"Nothing, huh?" he said, laughing. He knew what she was thinking. That his father was going out of town again, and the apartment would be empty...

A random junior stared at them as they walked down the hallway, but they were used to that. We were all used to that.

They make a great couple, the girl was thinking. *She's so nice and he's so adorable.*

Olivia smiled. *We do make a great couple,* she thought.

"We *are* pretty cute, aren't we?" Cooper asked the junior.

The girl turned bright red and hurried to class.

"You scared her away," Olivia said.

Cooper gave an exaggerated sigh. "I didn't mean to."

We did that a lot. Scared people. Freaked them out. Sometimes on purpose. It was just so easy.

"What do we have now?" Cooper asked.

"Lab. Then English. I finished the book last night."

The Age of Innocence was the next book on our twelfth grade reading list. Thank goodness. Last year, our English curriculum had been made up entirely of Paranormal Lit. *The Canterville Ghost*. *The Chrysalids*. *Macbeth*. Bloomberg High had been trying to give us books that reflected our experiences. We were pretty sure our lives had nothing to do with dystopian futures or Scottish castles, so we complained. This year, we had stuff like *The Age of Innocence, Jane Eyre*, and *Don Quixote*. Stuff that didn't reflect *anyone's* experiences.

"Was it good?"

"No," Olivia said, shaking her head. "It's depressing. Are you going to read it?"

"No," Cooper said, "I'm going to read the SparkNotes."

"Hah. You're such a rebel. You're lucky Ms Sheinmel can't read *your* mind."

"Very true," Cooper said, wagging his eyebrows. "She'd probably send me to detention for having inappropriate thoughts."

"You're having inappropriate thoughts about Ms Sheinmel?" Olivia joked, and this time they both laughed.

Olivia laughed a lot these days. Not because of anything in particular, but because she was happy. She was dating Cooper, and she was an Espie.

Two and a half years ago, she never would have believed that any of these things could happen to her. She had just moved to New York and she'd been painfully shy and overly anxious. She'd bitten and picked her thumbnails down to the quick until they bled.

Cooper had been totally out of her league. Not only was he one of the most loved guys at school, but he was with drop-dead gorgeous Mackenzie. They were the golden couple. No one ever imagined they would break up.

No one ever thought that a flu shot could give people ESP, either.

But things were good now. Things were so good, it was almost frightening.

Olivia couldn't help but wonder how long it would last. Nothing ever stayed the same, right? Things didn't stay good for ever. At some point the bubble would burst.

"There will be no bursting bubbles," Cooper said. "There will only be big, fluffy, bouncy bubbles. Speaking of which, do you have any gum?"

Olivia laughed again. "Yes," she said, and pushed the anxious thoughts out of her mind. These days she could do that. She handed Cooper a piece of Juicy Fruit.

Cooper never dwelled on the bad stuff. Which was pretty amazing after all the crap that had gone down with his parents. After his mom – and the rest of us – found out about his dad's affair, his dad had moved out and into a condo a few blocks away. There was a lot of fighting. Horrible divorce lawyers. Screaming matches. Frozen bank accounts. His dad was a jackass. His mom was bitter. Cooper and his little sister, Ashley, were always in the middle.

The divorce was the main reason he hadn't hooked up with Olivia during sophomore year. That, along with his breakup with Mackenzie, had tainted his view of relationships. He'd known there was something between Olivia and him, but he just hadn't been in the right frame of mind to start something new. They'd become friends instead. Good friends. They'd sat next to each other in class. Had lunch together. Hung out at parties.

And then, after junior year, his mom had remarried and moved to Warren, New Jersey. Cooper had spent the summer with her but, at the end of August, he'd moved in with his dad so he wouldn't be too far from school. The move had been rocky. He'd dealt with it, although not perfectly. He'd started smoking pot. A lot of pot. We'd warned him it could mute his ESP, but when he discovered that it didn't, he started smoking more. It relaxed him.

He liked being relaxed.

Olivia also relaxed him. It was nice to be with someone who didn't expect too much of him. Someone who liked him for who he was. Someone nice, who adored him.

They'd finally got together a week after he moved in with his dad.

It was two weeks before school started, and Cooper's father was out of town, as usual. Cooper was by himself. He was lonely. He was high.

He texted Olivia.

```
What are you up to?
```

He knew she'd spent the summer in the city.
She'd texted back straight away:

```
Just leaving the hospital.
```

Olivia had volunteered at Lenox Hill Hospital for the summer. She helped out by talking and reading to patients, taking samples to the lab and working at the desk in triage. Once, she even got to go with a cardiac patient to the cath lab and watch the procedure. All good training for med school. Plus, she loved helping people, which was why she wanted to be a doctor in the first place.

```
Cooper: Want to come by?
Olivia: Sure. Give me an hour.
```

When she'd got the text, she'd hoped, prayed, that tonight would be *the night*. Time was short. They had less than a year to be together as more than friends. Ten months and then...

Who knew what would become of us?

Olivia ran home to shower and put on something cute. *Tonight. Tonight. Tonight?*

When Cooper had opened his apartment door for her, he'd thought, *She's here!* Her cheeks were red from hurrying over, and her dark hair, wet from a shower and smelling of sweet shampoo, was pulled back in a tight ponytail.

He pulled her toward him and opened his arms.

It felt amazing.

She felt amazing.

"Livvie," he murmured. "Hi."

It was the way he said it. Soft and sweet, but husky at the same time.

"Hi." Her heart hammered. *Tonight? Is he? Will he? Finally?*

His heart started hammering, too. *Yes, Maybe I should.*

And he did. He turned his head toward her.

She closed her eyes and felt his lips press against hers. They were warm and soft. They tasted like smoke, but she didn't mind. Eventually, she felt him smiling and opened her eyes.

His eyes were twinkling. *Thanks for stopping by.*

Anytime. Do I get to come in?

That was eight months ago. There had been no games, no anything. They weren't just friends anymore; they were a couple.

They'd had two weeks before school started to get used to being together. Two weeks to try to develop a normal relationship. Well, relatively normal. They could hear each other's thoughts, which was obviously not normal. But eventually they got used to it. They learned to adjust, as normal couples did.

Not that it was a secret. We had run into them in the neighborhood. We were happy for them.

You're together!

No way!

It's about time!

Does Mackenzie know?

By the time Mackenzie bumped into them at the ice-cream truck parked on Greenwich, she was well aware.

Olivia's heart skipped a beat when she spotted her. *Will she care? Will he care?*

"I'm over her," he whispered. *Really.*

Olivia exhaled.

Mackenzie turned around. "Heard the news, you two," she said. "Congrats." *I'm happy for you. Really. Kind of.*

"After you, my lady," Cooper said now, opening the door for Olivia.

They were already three minutes late for Lab but Dr Dail never cared.

ESP Lab wasn't your typical kind of Lab. There was no dissecting frogs or setting fires with Bunsen burners. Instead, we practiced ESP, while Dr Dail gave out assignments and took notes.

This week, Olivia and Cooper were in a group with Nick, Courtney and Jordana. They were testing the effect that music had on transmission.

"Do, re, miiiiii…" Cooper sang.

"…fa, so, la, ti!" the twins responded. They were testing distance.

The twins were in a group with Levi, Mars, and Mona. Except Mars and Mona were skipping today, so it was just Levi and the twins.

"I'm taking ten steps back," Levi was saying, flashing his

super-straight, super-white smile as he moved back ten steps. He used to have bad teeth from all the candy he got from his parents' candy store, but once we became public, he'd gotten them straightened and whitened. "Okay, guys, what am I thinking? Is it still clear?"

"Ouch! I'll tell you what *I'm* thinking, numbskull," BJ said. "That was my foot you stepped on!"

BJ was in a group with Michelle, Sadie, Tess, and Mackenzie. BJ took off his shoe to examine his toe.

Tell Tess to kiss it, Levi thought. *Or suck on it.*

Gross, thought Michelle. Michelle had never kissed anyone on the lips, never mind on the toe. She was waiting for her Prince Charming.

"Thanks, but no thanks," said Tess.

"Stinky," Sadie said. "At least turn on the fan." Dr Dail had brought in a table fan to test the effect of air flow on transmission.

Morons, Pi thought. *They should test the air between their ears.*

"We can hear you," Nick said, casting her a look.

Pi was in a group with Brinn, Edward, Isaac and Anojah. They were testing mental shouting.

CAN YOU HEAR ME? Brinn hollered. Brinn was wearing the ridiculous bright white shoes she always wore, and what looked like a bra over the top of her shirt. She was eating a banana. She ate a lot of bananas. We all thought she *was* bananas.

"Loud and clear," said Anojah and then walked into a desk. She was always walking into things since wearing her glasses made the voices so much louder. Contacts caused problems too.

Anojah would have gotten laser eye surgery if Pi hadn't warned her that eye surgery was asking for trouble.

We kept at it for the next forty minutes.

We tried new things. We took notes. Dr Dail took notes. We were graded on participation.

"Great work, everyone," Dr Dail said, as she walked around the room. She wore her hair back in a tight bun, and extra large sunglasses to keep us out.

That's how we learned back in February about Pi getting recruited to be a spy. They *said* she was being recruited for a government think tank called Diamond, but one slip of Dr Dail's glasses and we knew the truth. Diamond was no think tank.

It was a secret program for spies.

Yes. After she graduated, Pi was going to be a spy for the US government. She would be sent on missions around the world where she would use her telepathy to gather information. Ten students from around the country had been chosen, all with special skills. She was the only one with extra-sensory skills.

Pi was, of course, thrilled. Out of all of us, she'd been the one chosen. That made her the best.

We all knew that wasn't true. Mackenzie was the one who could hear through walls. That, technically, made her the best.

Pi hated when we brought that up. We all knew that if Mackenzie just tried a little harder, she'd have been the one chosen for Diamond.

Also that Pi would have traded her perfect SAT score to hear through walls.

"Do you hear that?" Jordana asked Courtney.

"Hear what?" Courtney asked. *Brinn screaming?*

"No. That noise," Jordana said, putting down her nail file. "It's like a low humming."

"I don't hear anything," Courtney said.

Jordana swatted one ear and then the other. "Maybe I'm getting an ear infection."

"Maybe you should go see Nurse Carmichael," Dr Dail said.

The bell rang and we all piled out of the class.

It was nine and a half weeks before the senior cruise. Ten and a half weeks before prom.

April 1st, the beginning of the end.

Chapter Three
NUMBER ONE

"I really need new jeans," Courtney announced, so after school she and Jordana went to Jolie, a trendy new boutique in Tribeca.

"Hi," the salesgirl said. She stood up from the stool behind the cash register and put down her phone. "Let me know if I can help you find anything." *Damn. I really need to text Malena about tonight. But I guess I should pretend to be interested in these girls. They could be shoplifters.*

Bitch, Courtney thought.

Jordana smirked. *Wait for it...*

They look familiar, the salesgirl thought. *Have they been in here before?*

Courtney and Jordana started rifling through the clothes on the rack.

Are they famous? Maybe they're famous. Or their parents are famous. Who are they? If they're celebrity kids, then they must be loaded and can spend some cash. We've been open for two months and my commission still sucks. "The AG jeans are the best," she said in a fake-sweet voice. "I'm wearing them right now. They're sooooo comfy."

They make her ass look like a giant donut, Courtney thought.

Jordana giggled and flipped her hair.

Courtney picked up the jeans.

Omigod! I know who they are! They're those girls from that reality show!

Ding, ding, ding, Courtney thought.

I have to tell Malena! She's obsessed with that show. Huh. They're tinier than they look on TV.

Courtney cocked her hip. *Hear that? We're tinier.*

But the short one is way better looking.

"In her dreams," Courtney retorted.

"Thank you," Jordana said to the salesgirl.

The salesgirl turned white. *Omigod. They heard me.*

Jordana laughed. And then she gasped.

"What?" Courtney asked.

"My head is killing me," Jordana said, rubbing her temples. "I just got this insane pressure behind my eyes."

"But do you like the jeans? Should I try them on or not?" *They look awful on the sales-bitch but my ass is better, right?*

"They're great jeans," the salesgirl said, nodding vigorously.

"What the hell?" Jordana exclaimed. "Ow, ow, ow. Migraine!"

Jo! Answer me! My ass is better, right?

Jordana didn't answer. She just stared at the jeans.

"Hellllo?" Courtney pressed.

"What?" Jordana asked.

"I asked you a question!"

"No, you didn't."

"Yes, I did!"

"What was the question?"

"Are you kidding me?" *Is my ass better than the salesgirl's?*

"That was the question? You want to know if I'm kidding you?"

"Jo, concentrate! That's not what I asked."

"So ask it already," Jordana snapped. *Ask me the stupid question already!*

What's your problem? Can you not hear me? JO, CAN YOU HEAR ME?

Oh, I get it, the salesgirl thought. *They're having a mental conversation. They're thinking about something they don't want me to hear. Is it about me? Is it my mustache?*

Why is no one thinking anything? Jordana wondered.

I AM THINKING SOMETHING, Courtney's mind screamed. *Why can't you hear me?*

Jordana blinked.

I shouldn't have canceled my waxing appointment, the salesgirl thought. *My upper lip is like a forest. I need to reschedule.*

"Jordana, tell me you heard that! She's thinking ridiculous things about her mustache!"

The salesgirl gasped. "I knew it was bad!"

Jordana turned white. "Something is wrong. I can't hear a thing."

Nothing? Courtney thought.

Blink.

Blink, blink.

Nothing.

Jordana's ESP was gone.

Chapter Four
SHHHH!

The next day in homeroom we were seated in the horseshoe, waiting for Mr Jonas, when suddenly Jordana blurted: "Stop thinking! I can't hear you! You have to speak out loud!"

Mars, who along with Mona had decided to return to school today, stared at her with disbelief. "What do you mean, you can't hear anything?"

"It's my ESP," Jordana explained. She tilted her head to the left, then to the right. "I can't hear a thing. It's totally gone."

"But can you still hear talking?" Mona asked, raising her voice. "You can hear me now, can't you?"

Jordana looked liked she wanted to cry. "Yes, but not your thoughts. You don't have to shout."

Did she do something weird?

Like what?

Like stick a Q-tip in her ear?

It doesn't come from the ears!

Fine, her eye then.

Don't you think we'd notice if she had a Q-tip in her eye? She would have taken it out. She wouldn't have left it there, hanging out of her eyeball.

"She didn't stick a Q-tip in her eye!" Courtney exclaimed. "I was right beside her. One minute she could hear, and then she couldn't." She snapped her fingers for effect.

Well, she must have done something.

She didn't!

Maybe she took something.

Like what?

Jordana, did you take anything?

She can't hear you!

"Jordana, did you take anything?" Anojah asked, squinting across the room.

Jordana put her hands on her hips. "I don't do drugs! I'm a role model for young teenagers!"

We snorted with laughter.

"I didn't use anything," she insisted. "I know the rules. Besides, do you really think I'd risk *TMZ* or some random idiot with an iPhone filming me high? Are you kidding me?"

We had a pretty strict policy on drugs. We'd been warned that they might interact negatively with our ESP, and we took the warning seriously. Especially after what happened to Isabelle Griffin.

She was one of the original Espies. She'd partied a little too hard, took some weird designer drug and freaked out. Like totally freaked out. Like tried-to-jump-out-of-a-window freaked out. After that, she couldn't tell if she was hearing thoughts or having hallucinations. She took the antidote, pocketed the fifty thousand that came with it and transferred to another school.

She wasn't the only one to take the antidote.

Sergie Relov and Rayna Romero took it, too. He couldn't take the low-grade headaches that came with the ESP. She couldn't take the loud voices. She had a point. ESP got pretty noisy. We were used to it, though. We were used to the headaches, too. And the fact that our irises had developed an inexplicable purple tint.

We barely noticed any of that anymore.

And then there was Kermit. Oh, Kermit. We hardly even knew him. Like Mona, he was sick the day their class got their shots so he got his with us instead. Poor guy. He was a senior and thought studying for his SATs had made him bonkers. He got the antidote as soon as he heard about it.

Anyway. Back to drugs.

No one knew if it was the drug or the ESP that made Isabelle flip out, but we had decided not to take any chances.

We took mild stuff like Advil and Tylenol and had gallons of caffeine, but there was no blazing, blasting or getting fried. And no new prescriptions either, unless absolutely necessary. Not even another flu shot.

"Not even a little Mary Jane?" Levi asked, smirking at Cooper.

Pot's not a drug, Nick thought. *It's a herb.*

"You read my mind," Cooper said.

Jordana bit her lip. "Wait. Come to think of it, I did take some NyQuil. Could that have done it? Could it have actually wiped out my ESP?"

"I don't think so," Nick said. "Cold medicine is, like, 99 per cent alcohol. If alcohol did it, I'd be toast, too."

"I'm sure you'll snap out of it," Mona said. "Maybe it's like when you have a cold and go on a plane. You know, how your ears get clogged up?"

"So my brain is clogged up?"

"Exactly."

Just then Mr Jonas came in and we all sat down. "Good morning, everyone," he said solemnly. "What's new?"

Good game this weekend, Cooper thought. *I won a ton of cash.*

You still cheating those Jersey guys? Isaac thought.

It's not gambling when it's a sure thing, Nick thought.

Better not tell Mr Jonas, Levi thought.

Cooper laughed. *About my winnings? No way, he'd probably want a cut. We all know he's a party guy.*

Unfortunately, we had accidentally "overheard" one too many of Mr Jonas' hangovers.

Don't tell him about Jordana!

Why not?

It'll be a thing. We don't need any more "things".

It'll probably come back soon.

What if it doesn't?

Jordana was looking around the class, trying to figure out what we were saying.

"Nothing's new?" Mr Jonas asked, leaning against the front of his desk.

"Nothing," Pi said, and gave Jordana a meaningful look.

"Nothing," Jordana repeated.

By the time Friday's Lab rolled around, Jordana's ESP still hadn't returned.

"What should I do?" she wailed, walking into class with Mackenzie.

Olivia was right behind them. She sat down in her regular place next to Cooper, and picked at her thumbnail.

What if what happened to Jordana happened to her? She relied on her ESP. When you knew what people thought of you, you could adjust accordingly. Plus, she needed the rest of us to tell her about things she missed, stuff people wouldn't say out loud. Like if she had a muffin top. Or lipstick on her teeth.

You're not even wearing lipstick, Tess pointed out.

Are you saying she has a muffin top?

What's a muffin top? BJ wondered.

Olivia laughed and shook her head. No. She wouldn't worry about this. Jordana probably *had* done something silly, like taken too much Nyquil or stuck a Q-tip in her eyeball.

"What's going on?" Jordana asked Mackenzie when everyone was seated. "What are they all thinking? I can't stand this anymore! I hate not hearing!"

"You're not missing anything," Mackenzie replied. "Try not to stress. I'm sure it'll come back." She zipped up her sweater. It was always cold in Lab.

Jordana bit down on her lip. "Do you really think so?"

"Do you want it to?" Mars piped up.

"Of course I do! What kind of question is that? I can't hear anything! It's horrible! I'm a telepathic TV star! I can't not be telepathic!" She banged her fists on the table. "What kind of telepath doesn't have ESP?"

A fake one? Isaac offered.

Do you think she's just doing this for attention? Levi wondered, tilting back his chair.

Wouldn't we know if she was doing this for attention? Edward wondered back.

I'm glad it didn't happen to me, Isaac thought.

Me too, thought Olivia. Losing her telepathy would be like going deaf. No, it would be worse than going deaf. It would be like going blind.

Why is being blind worse than being deaf? Levi wondered.

No Xbox, Cooper thought.

Being blind is totally worse, BJ thought. *No boobs!*

You could still feel them.

Good point.

"Can you please talk out loud?" Jordana yelled. "I don't know what you're saying and it's driving me crazy!"

"It was just guy stuff," Sadie said. "Nothing important."

After two and half years of reading minds, we barely spoke

out loud when it was just us. Why waste the energy?

Jordana looked like she was going to cry. "Can we please get back to *me*? What if it's gone for ever? What happens to me then?"

"Then you become normal again," Mackenzie said. "Is that such a bad thing?"

You really want to be normal? Pi asked her.

Mackenzie didn't answer. She didn't have to. Two and a half years ago, we'd all refused the antidote. That said everything.

They'll probably switch her to 12A. They're short a student.

They're not going to switch her to another class at this point. It's April!

Some of us nodded and some of us shrugged.

"I don't want to be normal," Jordana whined. "I have to get it back. I just have to!" She turned to Pi. "Can't you do something?"

"What do you want *me* to do?" Pi retorted.

"You're supposed to be the genius here. Think of something!"

"Maybe you should have taken better care of yourself," Pi said, jutting out her chin. "Instead of spending so much time trying to be famous."

"OMG, shut up! Like you're any better?" Jordana shrieked.

Pi squared her shoulders. "I'm not trying to be famous." *I'm trying to be powerful.*

It's the same thing, Courtney thought.

Pi pursed her lips. *As usual, you don't know what you're*

talking about. Power is the ability to influence and control. Which is obviously something you'll never achieve. Anyway, the world doesn't really need an airhead with ESP.

"You're such a bitch," Jordana said. And she hadn't even heard the airhead part.

Chapter Five
WHAT IF IT HAPPENED TO ME?

Jordana's news put a damper on the weekend. Some of us thought her ESP would return. Some of us weren't so sure. But we were all thinking the same thing: *What if it happens to me?*

It was a beautiful Saturday, sunny and warm, the first nice weekend after a freezing-cold winter. We took off our scarves and left our coats at home, trading them for light jackets and sweaters.

Cooper and Olivia went to Square Diner for brunch. They even sat outside.

She ate her scrambled eggs and cheese, and watched him chew.

He smiled when he caught her looking at him. It was his classic smile, sweet and easygoing, and it always made her feel like melting. "Be right back," he said, going to the bathroom.

She knew she was lucky.

Then she thought about Jordana.

Olivia never wanted to go back to the way things were, pre-ESP.

A cloud passed over the sun and she felt a deep chill. She should have brought a warmer jacket. It was only April. What was she thinking? She hoped she wouldn't get sick.

Tess opened her eyes.

BJ's eyes were already open. *Now? Is now a good time?*

She couldn't help herself. She started to laugh and pushed him off her.

They were lying on his bed, his door closed. His beige sheets were piled in a heap on the floor.

"We're not doing it now!" She adjusted her bra and straightened her shirt.

"Why not? Today is the perfect day."

"And why is a random Saturday the perfect day?"

"It's not a random Saturday. It's the first week in April, the beginning of spring. Doesn't spring make you think of sex? It makes me think of sex."

"Everything makes you think of sex. Dried pasta makes you think of sex. You're incorrigible."

"Oh, good SAT word."

"I didn't get a high score for nothing."

"Maybe you were sitting next to Pi."

"Oh, please. You know I had my glasses on."

He nibbled her earlobe. "Can we get back to talking about sex?"

"You always want to talk about sex."

He laughed. "Talk about it. Do it. Both good options."

She rolled away from him. "You know we can't just do it."

"I know no such thing," he said.

"Yes, you do. If we do it, everyone will know."

"So what?" he asked. "It's not a crime."

"I don't want everyone knowing!"

He put his arm around her. "Sex is the world's worst kept secret. There has never been anything that is more public."

"What does that even mean?" Tess asked.

"My parents had sex. They had me. Your parents had sex."

She stuck out her tongue. "Once. Max."

"Your *grandparents* had sex."

Tess's mouth dropped in mock disgust. "Nana and Dede!"

"Yes, even Nana and Dede." He pulled her against him. "And I bet they liked it."

"You are seriously grossing me out," she said, and hit him with a pillow. "BJ, you know what the issue is. If we do it, the rest of our class will know within five minutes. Not even. They'll know thirty seconds after we walk into homeroom."

"Who cares if they know?"

"I do! It's personal!"

"But we know that Sadie did it. And Courtney. Even Cooper and Olivia. Even Pi did it, with that guy from Oxford. And what about Levi and all his groupies?"

Tess closed her eyes. "I do not need my memory refreshed on all that."

"Look at me, Tess," he said, and she did. "I love you, and if you're not ready, I understand. I don't want you to do anything you're not ready for. But please don't make any decisions based on the Espies. The only thing that matters is what *you* think."

She opened her eyes. She pressed her body against his.

"It's just…I don't know." *I didn't say I never want to do it. I just think we should wait until we graduate.*

Are you serious?

It's not that long. It's already been two and a half years. What's another couple of months?

Do you know how many days there are in a couple of months? How many hours? How many minutes? How many sec—

"I get the point, BJ." She sighed. *I just want it to be special, something that's just ours.*

He sat up. *Ding, ding! Why don't we do it over spring break? My parents are going to that adults-only resort in Jamaica.*

Her eyes widened. *The nudist club? Again?*

At least you know where I get my sex drive from.

Very true.

The point is we'll have the place to ourselves. Whatever we do, it'll be our secret. For a whole week.

Tess shook her head. *Someone will find out. I just know it.*

Not if we don't leave the apartment.

What about eating?

My parents are going to stock up before leaving. And we'll order in.

I'll still need to get to and from your apartment. What if someone sees me?

So you'll put on sunglasses and run. Come on, Tess. It'll be our secret. Just between us. For a whole week! He grinned at her. *Do you know how many days there are in a week? How many hours? How many minutes? How many sec—*

"I get it."

We'll give it a code name. How about The Plan?

"Now that's original."

Think about it! It's perfect!

I'll think about it. "I promise."

"You don't need to promise." He pulled her on top of him. "I'll be able to tell."

She sighed. "That's just the problem. As soon as spring break is over, they'll be able to tell, too." *Though who knows? Maybe our ESP will be gone by then, and no one will ever find out. If it can happen to one of us, it can happen to all of us.*

His raised an eyebrow. "You don't really want that, do you?"

"I don't know. Maybe." But the truth was, she liked being an Espie. She liked the closeness of the group. She just wished they weren't that close all the damn time.

Mackenzie spent the day walking around Soho.

Mackenzie loved window shopping. Every weekend she'd go to a different area in New York, try on clothes, and people-watch. She loved the boutiques, the shoe stores, the coffee shops. Sometimes she bought stuff, but usually she didn't.

She walked into a random coffee shop and waited in line.

She would miss New York when she went to California.

Stanford. She couldn't believe that's where she was going.

Her family had been as shocked as she was when she got in.

Her parents didn't expect much from her, and never had. She'd been born a preemie, at twenty-six weeks instead of forty. She'd required a lot of surgeries. Heart surgery. Kidney surgery. Eye surgery. Her parents hadn't thought she would make it. She'd been so small. Fragile. They'd assumed she'd always be a bit behind. Slower than her siblings. Jeff was still a senior at Stanford, and after graduating, Cailin was a financial advisor in Chicago. *They* were the smart ones. Mackenzie was the delicate one.

Mackenzie's parents never pushed her to work harder. They were happy with her Bs and Cs. Having telepathy had only confirmed what she had always known: her parents didn't expect much of her.

She didn't expect much of herself either.

She didn't even get an A in Lab, which was totally ridiculous since she was the only one of us with extra powers.

But Mackenzie wasn't much of a participator.

Mackenzie's mom was especially nervous about her going to Stanford. She'd said, "I'm so proud of you," but she'd thought, *I'm not sure she can handle it. The pressure might be too much. She's too fragile.* Then she closed her eyes when she remembered Mackenzie could hear.

She was one of the parents who wore sunglasses around the house. A lot. It wasn't that she was hiding anything. Mackenzie knew that from when her mom forgot to cover up. Her mother just liked her privacy. She liked being the mom. Her dad was the same, but forgot more often.

Mackenzie understood. If she had a kid who could hear thoughts through walls, she'd probably wear sunglasses, too.

Was she too fragile? Would the pressure get to her? Did she even want to go to Stanford?

"Hello? Hello?" the woman at the counter said. "Can I get you something or not?"

"Sorry," Mackenzie said, snapping back to reality. "I'll have a latte, please."

Dumb blonde, the woman thought.

Mackenzie sighed. Would losing her ESP really be so bad?

That weekend, Jordana and Courtney's reality show was being filmed in Chicago, but instead of going to the airport, Jordana called in sick. Even though the segment went well, the producers weren't pleased. The show was called *We Know What You're Thinking*, not *I Know What You're Thinking*. They were expecting two leads.

Courtney was stressed out the entire weekend. If the network found out that Jordana had lost her ESP, they would cancel the show. Then she got a flash. What if she got someone to replace Jordana? It would have to be someone seriously attractive. Maybe Mackenzie? Mackenzie was plenty hot, with her shiny hair and big eyes.

Not that Courtney really cared who the replacement was. As long as *she* wasn't the one being replaced.

* * *

Pi spent the weekend doing Sudoku and laps at the local pool. Not at the same time, obviously. Though if she could figure out a way to do it, she would. The swimming, she claimed, increased the blood flow to her head. The Sudoku stretched her brain.

Losing her ESP was not an option. She would not let that happen.

Chapter Six
SOMETIMES REALITY SUCKS

When we got back to school on Monday, Jordana still couldn't hear.

"I'm starting to really worry," she said in homeroom, as we waited for Mr Jonas. Mr Jonas was always late. Fact was, we made him uncomfortable. He usually seemed nervous, like he was worried his sunglasses would stop working and expose his secrets.

Like the fact that he had a nipple piercing.

Or that he liked to pick and eat his toenails.

Gross. Sometimes we wished his sunglasses never slipped.

"How long has it been?" Anojah asked, tripping over a chair.

"Almost a week," Jordana said, going a little crazy filing her nails. Back and forth and back and forth and back and forth. "Maybe it's not coming back."

"You shouldn't have taken the NyQuil," Pi scolded. "We told you not to take drugs. You shouldn't have risked it."

"I had a cold!" Jordana exclaimed. "I was congested!" She started pacing around the room. "What am I going to do? We're filming a spring break special! This weekend! In South Beach! Courtney, what are we going to do?"

"I don't know!" Courtney said, running her fingers through her hair.

"Are you going to tell the producers?" Tess asked.

"No!" Jordana said, narrowing her eyes and glaring around the horseshoe. "No one tells anyone! No one says a word. This is my life that's on the line! This is my show!"

"*Our* show," Courtney corrected.

"Maybe you should tell them you're sick," Mona suggested.

"I already did that. I can't do it again!"

"Just say you have mono," Levi said. "Or syphilis. I'll fill in for you. I'm moving to Miami, you know. I already know my way around."

No one wants to watch you running around in a Speedo.

His eyes lit up. *I'd get to wear a Speedo?*

Courtney turned to Mackenzie. *I've been thinking you'd make a great replacement. You interested?*

No thanks, Mackenzie thought. *Listening in on other people is not my idea of fun.*

It's not supposed to be fun. It's a job.

Brinn will do it, Dave thought. *She can wear her bathing suit on top of her clothes.*

Go to hell, Brinn thought. She took out a banana and started peeling.

Reality shows are for idiots, Pi thought.

Are you calling me an idiot? Courtney retorted.

Yes.

"Can you please speak out loud?" Jordana snapped.

Levi slapped his hand against his chest. "I would be amazing on TV."

"I saw you on *60 Minutes*," Cooper said. "You stuttered the whole time."

"Shut up! I was good."

"It's rude to make fun of the way people talk," Brinn mumbled, her mouth full of banana.

"Stop it!" Jordana said. "No one is replacing me! I signed a contract. Contracts are sacred. I know that for a fact. Before I became famous, I wanted to be a lawyer."

Michelle rolled her eyes. *And I want to be the queen of England.*

"So you'll break it," Nick said. "At the moment, it doesn't seem like you have a choice."

"I'll just have to do the show alone," Courtney said. *They don't really need two leads.*

"You cannot do it without me," Jordana said huffily. "I'm the star."

"Oh, please. We all know who the real star is. How many times have you trended on Twitter? I've trended three times!"

Jordana folded her arms across her chest. "I'm not canceling, and that's final."

BJ laughed. "How are you going to be on a show about reading minds when you can't read minds?"

"It's reality TV!" Jordana exclaimed. "Reality isn't really reality. They frankenbite everything we say."

"What the hell is frankenbiting?" BJ asked.

"That's not a real word," Pi said knowingly.

"I think—" Brinn started.

"Is so," Jordana interrupted. "It's when they cut and paste what you say so that you end up saying what they want you to say."

Levi looked confused. *So all the dumb stuff Jordana and Courtney say is actually made up?*

Shut up! Courtney thought. *It's not dumb.*

Jordana glanced from Courtney to Levi. "Stop. Thinking!"

"Maybe your telepathy will come back before then," Tess said.

"It'd better," Jordana said. She slumped down in her chair. "It'd really better."

BJ yawned. *The only thing more boring than watching reality TV is talking about it.* "What's everyone else doing for spring break?" he asked, thoughts of a naked Tess floating through his head. It was finally going to happen! Saturday!

Oops.

"Oooooooooooo," everyone said at once.

Tess's cheeks burned. *I did not agree to that yet!*

"What happened?" Jordana asked, looking around. "Somebody fill me in!"

Tess shot a look at BJ. *I hate this.*

So they know we're going to have sex, he thought. *It's no big deal.*

"It's natural," Cooper sang. "It's chemical…"

Please don't sing bad eighties songs, Mackenzie thought.

Bad? Are you crazy? Those songs are timeless! Cooper thought. *Come on, Mack, I bet you sing George Michael in the shower.*

Olivia's body stiffened. Where had *that* come from? Why was Cooper imagining Mackenzie in the shower?

Cooper turned to her, surprise on his face. *I wasn't! I was making a joke!*

Of course, as soon as he said it, he started imagining her in the shower. Her wet hair. Her wet body.

Mackenzie flushed.

Cooper shook his head. *Sorry! I'm sorry!*

Olivia cringed. She felt sick.

One of the drawbacks to having ESP was hearing your boyfriend or girlfriend think other people were cute. Or hot. Or whatever. It happened with all of us. It happened with Tess. It happened with BJ. It happened with Cooper. It happened with Olivia. When you were an Espie and dating an Espie, you had to make allowances.

But imagining your ex-girlfriend in the shower?

That was a bad one.

I sing in the shower, too, thought Sadie. *I have a terrible voice, though.*

I'm sure Dumbo doesn't mind.

Don't call him Dumbo!

Her boyfriend, an NYU student, was called Michael. But he

had really big ears so we all called him Dumbo.

BJ grinned. *So now that they know, do we still have to wait till Saturday?*

Tess began rocking back and forth on her chair. *We're not having sex, we're not having sex, we're not having sex...*

"We're not?" BJ said, making a hangdog face.

She stopped rocking and mentally elbowed him in the stomach. *I don't want to talk about it here!*

So that means we are *having sex?*

She's trying to psyche us out. We know you guys are going to do it.

Is she on the pill?

"None of your business!" Tess shouted.

Where are you guys going to do it? He'd better spring for a hotel ... His parents are going out of town — they're getting their naked on again at that nudist place ... That's so nasty ... So BJ and Tess are just doing it at home? Not classy ... Didn't you lose your virginity in the backset of a taxi? ... It was an Uber ... Better than Courtney. She lost it in Jersey ... It was the Jersey Shore ... BJ, you'd better get some candles. And roses. And music. And chocolate ... No, chocolate sauce ... Oooh, you're going to cover her in chocolate sauce? ... That's disgusting ... That's delicious ... So fattening ...

"I hate all of you," Jordana said, laying her head on her desk.

"I hate all of you, too," Tess said.

Except for BJ. You loooove BJ, and on Saturday you're gonna show him how much.

"Aaaaargh!" Tess screamed, and slammed her eyes closed.

Chapter Seven
BREAKING SPRING

Our last spring break had finally arrived. By Saturday evening, some of us were upstate, some in Florida, some in L.A. Mona was in Barbados. Sadie and Dumbo were in Chicago, where Dumbo's family lived. We wondered if they had big ears too.

The rest of were hanging out in Tribeca.

Mackenzie was home alone, and was feeling a little lonely. It was weird, though, how she found out about her parents' trip. On Friday when she got home from school, she got a text from her mom saying that she and Mackenzie's dad were taking a last-minute vacation to Newport and would be gone for the entire week.

Mackenzie was thinking about this as she looked at a fashion magazine on the couch.

Maybe it was a mini second honeymoon, she mused, as she

studied the slit on the side of a long red dress. A spur-of-the-moment, romantic decision. The more she thought about it, the more it made sense. Sometimes her parents embarrassed her, the way they carried on, always touching and hugging like a couple of horny teenagers.

On the other hand, it was totally irresponsible. Who texted their kids to say they wouldn't be home for a week?

Whatever. They'd probably just forgotten to tell her earlier.

She didn't mind having some time alone. It was nice and quiet.

She flipped the page and wondered if she had any spare dresses she could cut slits up the side of.

That evening, back at her place, Olivia was getting stood up.

Hey. Where are you?

She waited. Two minutes. Five minutes. Thirty minutes. No response. They were supposed to go for dinner at seven. Did she get that wrong? Maybe it was eight.

Cooper? Helllllllo?

She waited. She waited some more. It wasn't like him, standing her up. He might be absentminded – he crossed the street without looking both ways – but was never inconsiderate. She bit her thumbnail.

Could something have happened?

"I thought you had plans with Cooper," her mom said, walking into the living room.

"He's running late," Olivia replied, then went to her room to think in private.

Her breathing quickened.

Her mind raced.

She lay down on her bed.

Then she took a deep breath.

What was wrong with her? Why was she so freaked out? Was it because of what was going on with Jordana? Or because of that stupid shower joke?

She shook her head. She had to get over it. She was *not* going to revert to her pre-Espie anxious self. No way. Not happening.

Cooper was probably just stuck in his elevator. That happened a lot in New York. The elevators were old. Yes. He was stuck. That was it.

It was no big deal. It wasn't something to worry about.

She flipped onto her stomach.

Although if he were stuck in an elevator, he'd still call or text.

Why hadn't he called or texted?

Maybe he was trapped between the fourth and third floors. The elevator in his building didn't get cell service in that one spot. They always got disconnected between the fourth and third floors.

Or maybe his phone died? He always forgot to charge it. He could very easily be stuck in the elevator with a dead phone.

Yes. He was stuck in the elevator with a dead phone. That was it. He would call when he could. It wasn't a big deal.

She flipped back over.

But were there other people in the elevator? He could borrow a random person's phone and call her. But what if he didn't know her number by heart? He'd probably just entered her name in his phone.

No, he had to know her number. They were boyfriend and girlfriend.

He probably didn't know her number. That was the type of guy he was. A little lazy. He never made his bed. He didn't even have a lock on his locker.

He'd think, *Why should I memorize her number when it's on my phone?*

And he'd be right. Except for when he got stuck in an elevator with a stranger and had to use the person's phone.

Unless it wasn't a stranger.

What if it was Mackenzie? Mackenzie would be thrilled. Olivia knew that Mackenzie hadn't wanted to break up with Cooper. We all knew. Mackenzie still thought about him.

She thought:

He's so sweet.

I miss him.

If only I could get trapped in an elevator with him.

Okay, fine – Olivia had never actually heard Mackenzie think the elevator part, but it wouldn't surprise her. Maybe she'd asked the doorman to engineer a malfunction. Slipped him a twenty. But then Cooper would know. Would he care?

He might be flattered.

She bet he knew *her* number by heart.

Stop. Just stop, Olivia ordered herself. She was losing it.

Mackenzie had not orchestrated a stuck elevator to create a romantic moment with Cooper. She didn't even live in his building.

Olivia had to get a grip. She was spiraling and she knew it. She closed her eyes and took another deep breath. She had to stop thinking and take action. She sat up and texted him again:

Hey. What's up? Did you forget?

She waited for the bubble to show he was texting back. Nothing.

Maybe he had been hit by a bus.

No. Getting hit by a bus was statistically unlikely, but what about getting hit by a cab? There were millions of cabs in New York. And he never looked both ways before crossing the street! What if he had survived the elevator, stepped outside his building, crossed the street without looking and got run over by a taxi?

And now he was lying in a coma in the middle of the street. Or dead.

It could happen. One minute her dad was eating a corndog at the mall; the next minute he was lying on the floor in the middle of the food court. One minute you're alive, and the next minute you're six feet under in the Port Washington Cemetery.

Boom, boom. Snap of your fingers. Dead.

Her heart raced.

She looked out the window.

She wished she could see West Broadway. She listened for the sound of an ambulance. There was nothing. Maybe it was on its way.

Olivia turned away from the window in a panic. She had to get over there. Right away. She had to make sure he was all right.

She ran her fingers through her hair, grabbed her phone, and ran into the hallway.

"He's here?" her mom asked, looking up from her newspaper. *I didn't hear the buzzer.*

"No, I'm going to meet him."

"Okay. Have fun. Be careful." *I don't like her walking by herself at night.*

"It's not night. It's evening."

"It's going to be night." *What if someone sneaks up on her? Although she would hear them sneaking up on her. But even if she hears them, that doesn't mean she'll get away in time—*

Olivia's mom never bothered wearing sunglasses in the house. She was used to Olivia hearing her every neurotic thought. She liked it.

"Mom! Stop worrying!" Olivia ordered, ignoring the irony. She grabbed her purse and jacket. "If Cooper calls, tell him I'm on my way. I'll text you when I get there."

Her mother's eyebrows shot up. "Cooper never calls the landline."

"True," Olivia said. He probably didn't know that number,

either. But there was no time for explanations. She had to go! Cooper was lying in a coma and she was wasting time!

"Bye, love you," she called, and ran out the door.

It took her precisely nine minutes to sprint to Cooper's.

"Hey, Carlos," she said to his doorman, as she approached the building.

"What's shaking, Olivia?"

"Is Cooper home?"

"Yup," he said. "His dad is away again but Cooper's there. Go on up."

"Thanks," she said, and rode the elevator to the seventh floor.

When the elevator stopped, she got out, went to his apartment, and pushed open the door. Cooper never locked it. He figured, why bother? The doormen only let up people he deemed worthy.

"Hello?" she called.

No one answered.

Oh, God. She was right. Something had happened.

"Hello?" she called again. "Cooper?"

Still no answer.

As she approached his room, she heard music. Soft music.

He was home. And listening to music. What the hell?

Was there someone in the room with him? Freaking Mackenzie! Had she wooed him back to his room post-elevator crisis?

His door was closed. Olivia knocked.

No response.

She knocked again. "Coop?"

Nothing.

Oh, God. He *was* dead. Either dead, or in bed with Mackenzie.

Or both.

She turned the handle, opened the door.

The blinds and window were open, cold air blowing into the room. She saw a lump under the covers. A single, large lump. Whew. He wasn't with Mackenzie.

Although he could still be dead.

Tentatively, she approached his bed. "Cooper?"

She heard him breathing. He could still be in a coma, though.

She placed her hand on his arm. "Cooper?"

His eyes flew open. "Liv?"

"You're alive."

He sat up. "Did I...Were we supposed to...?"

"You fell asleep?"

He stretched and smiled sheepishly. "Yeah."

"You forgot we had plans?"

"No. I took a nap and slept for" – he glanced at his clock radio – "wow, four hours."

"Are you getting sick?"

"Maybe."

She sniffed. And then sniffed again. The room reeked. "Are you high?"

"Um..." *Yeah.*

You got high, took a nap, and slept through our date?

"I had a late night, but it was worth it. I won a bundle. Come cuddle?"

"No." She was annoyed. He'd been playing poker again, in some kid's garage. Alan something-or-other lived down the street from Cooper's mom and went to Kennedy High. Truth was, she hated his gambling more than his smoking. She thought it was extremely dangerous. What if the Jersey guys realized he was an Espie? They'd be pissed. They might beat the crap out of him.

Besides, it was just plain stealing when you could read the other players' minds. And it wasn't like he needed the money.

"It's for fun," he'd tell her.

"I thought you were visiting your mom," she finally said. "You didn't tell me you were going to a game."

He shrugged. "I went later."

Isn't he worried about getting caught?

No. He isn't.

So now you think about yourself in the third person?

Cooper laughed.

I wish you would stop. This wasn't the first time she'd asked, and as usual, he laughed it off.

"What can I say?" he replied, giving her his classic smile. "I like winning."

She looked at his tired face. It could be worse, she supposed. At least he wasn't dead. Or in bed with Mackenzie.

"I'd rather be in bed with Mackenzie than dead," he said, and pulled her on top of him.

"Oh, shut up."

He wrapped his arms around her.

"You stink of pot."

He nodded sleepily. "Sorry."

They had the place to themselves. They were in bed. The last of her annoyance evaporated like smoke.

Chapter Eight
THE PLAN

Tonight was the night.

They'd stopped talking about it, but they knew it was going to happen. Naturally, we did, too. It was all they could think about.

Even though the secret was out, they were sticking to The Plan. They were determined to ignore us the entire spring break. That way, they'd have a week to themselves. An entire week without having to listen to us tease them.

They were in the living room, both wearing silk robes.

When BJ first handed Tess the robe, her mind screamed, *I'm so not wearing your mother's robe!*

He laughed. *It's not my mother's. I bought it for you.*

She kissed him on the cheek. "You bought me a robe?"

"I got us *matching* robes."

"You are such a geek."

"Yes, but a romantic geek."

"Very," she agreed. "And I brought us champagne and strawberries."

But now, naked under the silk robe, she was feeling nervous. She wanted to open the champagne immediately. Chug the whole bottle.

"I love champagne and I love strawberries," BJ said. "But why do they go together? I don't get it. Are you supposed to dip the strawberries in the champagne?" *It's really happening. We're going to have sex.*

"I think the strawberries bring out something in the champagne," Tess said. "Or maybe the champagne brings out something in the strawberries." *No idea, can't think, can't think. We're going to make love. We're going to have sex!*

"Let's open that champagne." *She's nervous. I'm nervous. Are we nervous?*

"Good idea," she said. *Yes, we're nervous.*

"You know what I've always wanted to do?" His eyes lit up.

She grinned. *Have sex with me?*

"Besides that. I've always wanted to open champagne with a sword."

She raised an eyebrow. *Really? Now that's weird.* "You have a sword?"

"No, but I have a steak knife. You're supposed to slash off the top." He made a slashing movement. "Haya!"

I'd rather you didn't.

"Maybe not," he said.

"Let's just Google how to open champagne."

"I know how to *pop* it," he said, with an exaggerated wink.

No virginity-popping puns, she begged.

"Sorry! Couldn't resist. Let's go onto the balcony."

She followed him out and watched him struggle with the bottle. Eventually the cork went flying over the railing and into the night.

I hope that didn't hit anyone, he thought.

"I don't hear screaming."

He poured two glasses. It bubbled over, spilling onto the balcony floor.

"To us," she said.

"To us," he repeated.

They both took sips. Big, long sips. And then more sips.

She let the bubbles pop on her tongue. She'd had champagne before, but never with the Hudson River spread out below her. Never while wearing a silk bathrobe.

"I want tonight to be perfect," she said.

"It already is," he replied.

"Do you think we should wear our sunglasses?" she asked.

No! That's crazy. We love each other. I don't even want us to close our eyes. I want to hear everything you think.

Tess's heart sped up. She loved him. She really did. Sometimes she didn't think she had ever loved anyone this hard and this much in her whole life.

She put down her glass. "Let's do this."

His eyes lit up. "Yeah?"

"Yeah." *Also, it's freezing out here*.

He swooped her up in his arms and carried her to his bedroom.

How romantic, she thought.

You ain't seen nothin' yet.

She started to laugh the second they went into his bedroom. He'd lit candles everywhere, even on top of his Xbox. Soft music was playing in the background. The bed was made and, wait – were those rose petals on his sheets? Rose petals – and a box of condoms.

Cheesy? he thought, looking worried.

She blushed. *It's perfect*.

BJ went first. He slipped off his robe and let it fall to the floor.

Tess slipped off hers.

They had seen each other undressed before – parts, at least – but they had never both stood there completely exposed.

You're so beautiful.

She blushed. "You're not so bad yourself."

She stepped closer and pressed her body against his.

It's finally going to happen, he thought for the hundredth time.

She laughed. "Yes, BJ, it's finally going to happen."

Marvin Gaye's 'Let's Get It On' cooed from the speakers. They stared into each other's eyes.

You totally made a sex playlist, didn't you?

Totally.

He lifted her onto the bed, then pulled her on top of him. She smelled of lilac shampoo and rose petals; his skin felt cool and smooth against her own.

I love you, Tess.

I love you, too.

Chapter Nine
WHAT YOU DON'T KNOW CAN'T HURT YOU

Mackenzie got out of the subway on 59th and Lexington. It was now Thursday afternoon, her week of leisure almost over. She was planning to spend a few hours wandering down Madison Avenue, when she bumped right into her mother.

"Mom? What are you doing here? I thought you were in Newport. Did you get back early?"

Her mother froze in her tracks. *Oh, no.* Then she pushed her sunglasses from her perch on her head down over her eyes.

Had her mom just blocked her? "Mom? I don't understand. I thought you were coming back tomorrow." Why was her mom pretending to be in Newport when she was really in New York? "What's going on? Why are you here? Where's Dad?"

They were standing on the corner in the middle of the day.

Annoyed tourists and New Yorkers pushed around them, but neither of them moved.

"I needed to think," her mom said. Her face was flushed. "I was taking a walk."

"I don't understand. Why aren't you in Newport?"

"I…" Her mom stopped talking.

"Mom! What happened?"

No reply.

"Can you take off your sunglasses, please?"

"No."

Mackenzie's heart pounded. A taxi beside them let out a loud honk. "You're scaring me. Please tell me what's going on. Tell me what's going on!"

"Mackenzie…" her mom started. "I don't know how to say this."

"Say what? Just tell me!"

"I'm… I'm sick."

Mackenzie's mouth went dry. "You're sick? What kind of sick? Like the flu?" she asked, even though every bone in her body knew it wasn't the flu.

"No," her mom said. "Cancer."

Mackenzie felt like she'd been punched in the stomach. "You have cancer?"

Her mom nodded. "In my throat."

"Are you…" *Going to die* was what Mackenzie wanted to ask, but stopped herself just in time. She could not ask her mom that. That was not what you asked someone who was sick. And she was afraid of the answer. If her mom said yes,

Mackenzie would collapse right there on the sidewalk. She would just fall down. People would have to step over her. Or maybe she would simply dissolve.

She remembered something that people with cancer talked about. What they'd talked about when her grandfather had stomach cancer years ago. Stages. Yes. Stages. She was supposed to ask about stages. Stage one, stage two, stage three. "What stage is it?" she asked.

"They think it's stage two," her mom said. "I need more tests to be sure."

Mackenzie didn't remember how many stages there were. Ten? Two out of ten wasn't bad. It was pretty good, actually. Wasn't it?

"You're going to get better, right? It's treatable, right?"

Her mom was still wearing her sunglasses. Mackenzie could see her reflection in the lenses. Suddenly, desperately, she hoped her mother would never take them off.

"It should be," her mom answered.

Should be? Mackenzie's eyes filled with tears.

"Oh, sweetheart," her mom said. "Please don't cry. I'm going to beat this, you'll see." She managed a small smile. "Come, have lunch with us. I was just on my way back to the hotel. Your dad's there now, checking us out."

Mackenzie stared at her. "The hotel? You're staying at a hotel?" And, finally, understanding set in. "You were hiding out," she said. "You didn't want me to know."

"Worry. I didn't want you to *worry*, and I was afraid something would slip. I just hated the idea of worrying you."

Mackenzie's mom reached into her purse for a tissue. "You know that sore throat I was complaining about? Well, last Friday, I finally went to the ENT. He told me I needed a biopsy. But I didn't want to say anything until I got the results back. I didn't want to worry you for nothing."

"Except it's not nothing," Mackenzie said. "When were you going to tell me?"

"I just got the results this morning. I've been walking around in a daze. Don't be mad, Mackie, I can't take it."

Mackenzie closed the gap between them and hugged her mom tightly. Tighter than she ever had in her life.

Chapter Ten
ANOTHER ONE BITES THE DUST

Spring break went by quickly, like vacations always do.

For most of us, anyway. It did not go by quickly for Jordana or Courtney.

Jordana's telepathy hadn't returned, but she went to South Beach anyway. "We'll shoot around it," she'd claimed, though not to the producers. She couldn't risk them firing her, so she'd come up with a plan: Courtney would secretly text her things she thought Jordana should know.

Like how the woman in the leopard-skin pants had no belly button.

Or how the man in the taxi wasn't wearing underwear.

Or how the girl at the convenience store had stashed five bags of gummy bears in her bra and munched on them throughout the day.

Jordana thought it was brilliant. We thought it was risky, since Courtney had to text it all without looking. Jordana would then sneak a quick glance in her purse and read:

```
Girl im panntts ha np bwell brton
```

Also, it rained. Every afternoon. It was hard to go to the beach when it rained, so the producers made them go early – like 7 a.m. – to avoid the afternoon showers. Ugh. Who wanted to get up at 7 a.m. on spring break?

Besides Pi, that is. She was an early riser.

Fortunately for Courtney and Jordana, no one else wanted to go the beach at 7 a.m. either, so the beach sessions were canceled. But all was not lost. The evening footage was great. They went to nightclubs and trendy restaurants, which gave them plenty of opportunity to listen to people. Of course, their subjects had to sign a waiver saying they could appear on camera. They also had to sign a second waiver allowing their thoughts to be used. Last season, someone had sued for copyright infringement. Most people, however, never even read the waiver. They heard "TV show", signed, and fixed their hair.

Since the texting solution wasn't really working, Jordana had to resort to old-fashioned guessing. It was shocking how wrong she was 99 per cent of the time.

"Tell us what the girl in the sarong was thinking when she was standing next to you," the producer asked Jordana.

"She was, um, thinking about how cute her boyfriend is

and hoping I wasn't trying to flirt with him," she answered with authority.

Courtney would have laughed if it weren't so far from the truth. The girl had been wondering how a butterface like Jordana had landed her own TV show. Meaning the girl reckoned Jordana had a great body – but not a great face. Better that Jordana hadn't heard the details.

The smart thing would have been for Jordana to lie low. But did she? No, she did not. She tried to steal every scene. It was seriously annoying.

Courtney knew she could expose her. It would serve her right. But it would risk everyone thinking they were both frauds. And she couldn't risk that.

Meanwhile, back in New York, Tess and BJ didn't go anywhere. They were having sex. A lot of it. They didn't even go out for dinner. They stayed home and darted back and forth between their apartments, Diamond-style, hoping no one would see them.

Cooper spent the vacation partying. His dad was out of town on business, so his apartment was party central for all the Espie guys who'd stayed in the city. Nick. Levi. The twins. All except BJ. Who was, um, busy.

Olivia came and went. She didn't smoke with them. She'd never tried it and didn't want to, especially now that her anxiety was making a comeback.

No. She had to squash it. She'd had one spiral, that was it.

She wasn't going to start obsessing again. There was no reason to. She still had Cooper. She still had ESP.

Besides Jordana, we all did.

At least, until the last Saturday of the break.

At precisely 11:14 p.m. we got a group text from Anojah.

```
Anojah: Guys?
Levi: What up?
Michelle: You're back?
Anojah: I got back on Thursday. But
something just happened. I can't
hear anymore.
Edward: WTF?
Mars: What do you mean?
Anojah: I can't HEAR anymore. The
telepathy is gone.
Isaac: No shit!
Nick: Shit.
Courtney: Totally gone?
Anojah: Like Jordana gone.
Olivia: Oh, no!
Pi: Did you take NyQuil?
Anojah: I took nothing. I got a
crazy headache and then it just
disappeared.
Jordana: That's what happened to
me! I knew it wasn't from drugs!
Michelle: How was Miami?
Jordana: Great. I nailed it.
Pi: Please focus. This is SERIOUS.
```

Michelle: What do we do?

Courtney: If it happened to two of us, it could happen to all of us.

Olivia: Do you think it will happen to all of us????

Michelle: Would that be so bad?

Olivia: Yes!

Edward: YESSSSSSS

Cooper: sjj

Michelle: What? Cooper?

Jordana: Did he fall asleep on his phone?

Cooper: Meant hjh

Cooper: idk

Michelle: What is hjh?

Brinn: What is idk?

Olivia: He means he doesn't know if it'll happen to us or not.

Courtney: Cooper, are you high?

Jordana: When is he not high?

Levi: Hey, Jordana, should you still be in this group? Isn't it just for Espies?

Jordana: Screw you.

Levi: You wish.

Jordana: HAHAHAHAHA Seriously? I just threw up in my mouth.

Anojah: Should we call the people

at the Centers for Disease Control
and Prevention?

All the answers flooded our phones at once: No! ...
NOOOOO! ... YES! ... Why? ... No one says a
word! ... We can't tell anyone!

Pi: Let's talk about it in person.
Tomorrow.
Isaac: Sunday?
Nick: It's vacation!
Anojah: Guys! It's an emergency.
Pi: Yes! We need to decide what to
do.
Levi: She means SHE'LL decide what
to do.
Dave: LOL
Daniel: LOL
Anojah: I AM FREAKING OUT.
Courtney: Does anyone else think
it's adorable that the twins
accidentally send identical texts?
Dave: ☺
Daniel: ☺
Jordana: You did that on purpose.
Daniel: We'll never tell.
Dave: We'll never tell.
Tess: Can someone please suggest a

meeting place?

Isaac: How about Cooper's? His dad is away.

Cooper: kgh

Courtney: Olivia, does it stink in there? I can't run around the city smelling like I'm from Colorado.

Nick: It smells delicious. Chill.

Pi: We'll meet at Cooper's. Tomorrow. 3 p.m.

Michelle: Is everyone back already?

Sadie: Hola! I got back last night.

Mars: Mona's still in Barbados.

Brinn: I'm back.

Courtney: I didn't even know Brinn was gone.

Cooper: Mackenzie, you there? Tess? 3 p.m. okay?

BJ: We're coming.

Levi: Right now? On the phone?

Courtney: Does that mean they did it?

Pi: Our future is at stake, and you're talking about sex? Just be there, okay? We'll fill in the no-shows later.

Some of us texted "Byes", some of us "Laters".

Pi just disconnected.

She couldn't understand why we weren't taking this seriously. But it wasn't *our* future she was worried about. Without her ESP, she could kiss her future spy job goodbye.

Chapter Eleven
HELP!

BJ took Tess's hand. "Are you ready?"

"I guess," she said. "How long do you think it will take them to find out?"

"Ten seconds?"

"Maybe they forgot about it," Tess said. "Let's try not to think about it."

"Hah! Like that ever works. And who cares?"

"I do," she said. "You know I do. We should try one of the techniques."

"Like unnecessary pain?" BJ asked, looking worried.

"Exactly."

"Like what? You'll start elbowing me in the stomach?"

"That might be a little obvious. I was thinking we could just pinch each other."

He pinched her butt. "Did that work?"

"That made it worse," she said. "Now I'm thinking about sex."

"Hah!"

"Let's just hum," Tess said. Back when our ESP was new, we discovered that humming, like pain, could mask our thoughts by giving us something else to focus on. But how long could you keep humming? "No, let's wear our sunglasses."

"For the rest of our lives?" BJ laughed.

"No, just for the rest of senior year."

"We could," he answered. "But then we won't be able to hear their thoughts, either. Is that what you really want?"

Tess sighed. "No, I guess not." Fact was, she liked the closeness, when it didn't get *too* personal. They were all in the same boat. If anything, ESP was a great equalizer. "Okay, let's do this," she said, taking a breath.

BJ squeezed her hand and the elevator opened.

As usual, Cooper's door wasn't locked. The living room was enormous, and since Cooper's dad was always out of town, it was the perfect place for Espie meet-ups. The room was already full.

"Hellooo," Cooper sang, seeing them coming in. "Take a seat. We're just about to start. How was your vacation?"

BJ braced himself as he and Tess sat down. *Don't think about it don't think about it don't think about it...*

We had sex! Tess mentally screamed. *Oh, no! No, no, no, no...*

We froze.

And then: "Mazel tov!"

"Finally!"

"How was it?"

Mars gave BJ a high five.

"Boo-ya!" Cooper said.

Tess was beet-red. *You could at least pretend you hadn't heard me. That would be the decent thing to do.*

You shrieked it!

Why is everyone making such a big deal? We knew it was going to happen.

And now we want details!

"I'm not giving any details!" Tess yelled.

I hope they used condoms.

Did they use the chocolate sauce?

You guys are such pervs, Michelle thought.

"I don't want to talk about this!" Tess yelled.

"Then you shouldn't have brought it up," Courtney said, flipping her hair.

Pi cleared her throat. "Is everyone here?"

We looked around the room. We counted. There should have been twenty of us. Nineteen seniors and Mona. We were missing one person.

"Where's Mackenzie?" Courtney asked. "Tess?"

"I don't know. I haven't heard from her all week."

Sadie gave Tess a knowing look. *You were getting busy.*

Tess felt a little guilty. Mackenzie was her best friend. Best friends were supposed to tell each other everything, right? She took out her phone and texted:

```
Hey! You coming? Everything OK?
```

Yes, she felt guilty, but Mackenzie hadn't reached out to her, either. She hadn't texted once over the week. Where was she?

A text popped up:

```
Can't make it.
```

"She can't make it," Tess read out loud.

"She has something more important to do?" Jordana snapped.

I don't know! Tess thought. Why didn't she know? She felt bad. All week she'd been enjoying her love bubble while something was up with her best friend.

"We're starting without her," Pi announced. "Anojah, can you tell us what happened?"

Anojah nodded. "I had a bad headache," she said. "My vision was a little blurry and then—"

"Your vision is always blurry!" Levi said.

"Let her finish, please," Pi said.

"—and then the headache got worse and then suddenly I couldn't hear the voices anymore."

"That's exactly what happened to me!" Jordana called out.

"Where were you when it happened?"

What difference does that make?

She's being thorough.

What if she was in the bathroom?

What voices would she be listening to in the bathroom?

Mr Clean? Cooper thought.

Everyone who could still hear laughed.

"What's so funny?" Jordana asked. "We can't hear you. You have to talk out loud or it's not fair."

Poor baby.

"They're just making stupid jokes," Pi said. "Anojah, can you answer the question? What were you doing when it happened?"

She crossed her legs on the Persian carpet. "I was eating dinner with my parents."

"What were you eating?"

"My mom made chana masala."

"Hmm. Do you know what ingredients she used?"

"You think it was something I ate?"

Pi shrugged. "Maybe. I don't know."

Do you think her mom poisoned her?

Why would her mom poison her?

I think my mom has tried to poison me.

"I'm not saying her mom tried to poison her," Pi said. "I was wondering if it was a new recipe."

"It wasn't," Anojah said.

No one said anything. But we were all thinking the same thing: *Crap.*

I don't want to lose it!

What can we do?

Olivia started to panic. She had known her life was too good to be true. *I knew it I knew it I knew it…*

I cannot lose it, Pi thought. *I cannot let this happen.* "I need to fix this," she said, looking around the room.

No shit, Einstein.

Who died and made her the boss?

"Maybe it's like baby teeth," Cooper said, from his spot on the edge of his couch. "They're just going to fall out. We can't stop it."

Are you high right now? That doesn't even make sense. You get new teeth. We're not getting new teeth!

Cooper snorted. *Then it's like going bald.*

You can get a hair transplant, Nick thought.

Jordana slammed her fists on the floor. "Can you guys talk? I can't hear!"

"Actually, it's kind of peaceful," Anojah said. "It's so quiet. I like it. And I got contacts! I can finally see!"

"I don't like it at all," Jordana whined.

"Maybe it's like the first time you get your period," Sadie said.

"Ew, gross!" Edward said.

"Oh, grow up," Courtney said.

"I'm serious," Sadie went on. "They say the earlier you get it, the longer you get to keep it. Were Jordana and Anojah the last ones to get their ESP?"

"I think I was the sixth," Jordana said. "Or maybe the seventh."

"I don't remember," Anojah said.

"Maybe we should get another flu shot," Courtney suggested. "Maybe it will boost our ESP."

"What about the interactions?" Mona asked. "It's still on our list of no-nos, isn't it? Because if it's not, I want one. I had the flu last year, and it was miserable."

Brinn started mumbling. "Actually, I think—"

"I think it's a good idea," Olivia interrupted. "So many people come through the hospital with flu. Do you know how many people die from it every year in this country? Over thirty thousand!"

"It's still a drug," Isaac pointed out. "We inject it into our system. We don't know what could happen."

"Pi, is there an ESP booster?" Courtney asked. "Something that won't cause an interaction?"

"How should I know?" Soon, once she joined the CIA for real, she would know everything. But not yet.

And not ever if she lost her ESP.

"We should ask Dr Dail," Dave said. "If anyone can help us, she can."

"I'm with Dave," Daniel said. "I think we should ask her."

Pi shook her head. "She doesn't know anything."

You're still mad that she thinks Mackenzie has better ESP than you.

I am not! Well...maybe I am. But that's beside the point. "Dr Dail doesn't care what happens to us. How do we know she won't just try and inject us with the antidote? Besides, she'll have to tell someone, and you know what happens once news starts spreading. Do we want everyone to know? What if our colleges find out? If they think we're losing our ESP, what's to stop them from pulling our offers?" *She's the one who recommended me to Diamond! There's no way she can know.*

"Can they do that?" Sadie asked. "Is that even legal?"

"Of course they can," Pi snapped. "They'll base it on a misconduct charge or academic dishonesty – something lame like that. Which is why we have keep it a secret and fix this fast." She stared at Jordana. "Do you really want to have to take finals?"

Like many high schools, Bloomberg High exempted students from final exams if they had a high grade point average. But Principal Roth had extended the criteria to include kids with ESP. We figured he didn't want to take a chance on any of us failing and having to spend another year in his school. Being principal for Espies wasn't easy. Our last one, Nathan Michaels, had resigned after six months.

Jordana paled. "I can't take those exams! I haven't studied all year!"

"What do you care?" Edward said. "You're a TV star."

"Not if anyone finds out I lost it! They'll kick me off the show! Omigod, am I going to have to go to college?"

"Did you even apply?" Sadie asked.

"No. Why? Does that matter?"

"We are not contacting Dr Dail," Pi proclaimed. "And that's that."

Excuse me?

She's so bossy.

I don't trust her.

"But we have to do something!" Jordana cried. "We have to think of a way to bring it back!"

Sadie turned to Pi. "You're the smart one. Figure something out."

At least she recognizes who's in charge, Pi thought. *Not like these other morons.*

We can hear you, Pi.

"Don't worry," she said, looking out Cooper's living room window. "I'll fix this." *I have no idea what to do.*

Everyone stared at her.

"We're screwed," Levi said.

"I said I'd fix it," Pi snapped, and then started humming loudly in her head. But she needn't have bothered. Her mind was blank.

Chapter Twelve
THE MONSTER IN THE ROOM

It was Monday morning, the first day back at school after spring break. Mackenzie was staring blankly into her locker when she heard, "There you are!"

She turned around to see Tess standing there.

"Where have you been hiding?" Tess asked. "Why weren't you at the meeting?" *I have news! Lots of it!*

Mackenzie blinked back tears. *My mother has cancer.*

Tess froze. "What?"

She has cancer. In her throat.

Holy shit. That makes no sense. She's not even a smoker.

I know.

What stage?

Two. Maybe.

That's not as bad as it could be, right?

I guess.

I mean, it's not… It doesn't mean she's going to die.

She could.

We all die eventually.

Mackenzie closed her eyes. "Can you stop?"

Tess hugged her friend. "This isn't coming out right. I don't know what to say. I'm sorry."

Mackenzie sighed. "Me, too. I just found out on Thursday. She didn't want me to know. So she checked into a hotel. A hotel! How crazy is that? Just to make sure I wouldn't find out."

It did seem kind of crazy. "I'm sure she just didn't want you to worry," Tess said.

Mackenzie scrunched up her face. "Well, guess what? I'm worried."

"Of course you are," Tess said. "So, what happens next?"

"Surgery."

"No chemo?"

"Maybe," Mackenzie said. "They don't know yet." She turned around and leaned her forehead against the locker. "I can't believe she has to go through this."

"It sucks." Tess rubbed Mackenzie's shoulders. "I guess that's why you've been MIA? You didn't want to talk about it?"

"At least I won't have to actually say anything. They'll find out on their own. The second I step into homeroom."

"You can always wear sunglasses."

"Or check into a hotel." Mackenzie turned back around.

"Maybe I will. Wear sunglasses, I mean. They don't have to find out this minute, do they?" She pulled hers out of her bag.

"I guess I should put mine on, too," Tess said. "Let me just stop at my locker—"

"No, never mind," Mackenzie said. "Now or later, what's the difference?" She put away her glasses and looked back at Tess. "So, what happened at the meeting?"

Tess shook her head. "Forget I said anything. Just concentrate on your mom."

"No, tell me," Mackenzie insisted. "I want to know what's going on."

Tess sighed. "Did you read the texts?"

"No, none of them."

"Anojah lost her—" Tess stopped talking out loud. *Telepathy. She lost her telepathy.*

She did?

Yeah.

How come?

We don't know.

So now we're down two?

Yup. Tess frowned. *Scary, right? What if we all lose it?*

Mackenzie shrugged. *I don't know if that would be the worst thing.*

Really? You want to give it up?

I don't know. Maybe it's better not knowing everything. Easier, anyway.

Despite her sex life being as public as Twitter, Tess couldn't imagine losing her ESP. The ability to hear thoughts had to be the best writer's tool ever. Plus, she liked knowing everything about BJ. She liked that he knew what she was thinking, too. They were intimate. They were a unit. One amazing unit. *Especially in bed.*

"Oh my god!" Mackenzie exclaimed. "The Plan! You did it!" *Why didn't you tell me?*

I haven't spoken to you!

"I knew it! I wanted to call you, but I was afraid of, um, interrupting you. I knew you wanted your privacy." She shook her head. "Wow, I bet the others tortured you on Sunday."

Tess blushed, like she did every time she thought about the group's reaction to The Plan.

"Stop staring," she said.

"They say you look different after your first time. I'm trying to see if you look different."

Tess blushed again. "Shhhh!"

And...?

Tess smiled. *And it was amazing.* And because she couldn't help herself, she added, *The second time, anyway. The first time lasted three and half seconds.*

For the first time in days, Mackenzie laughed.

Chapter Thirteen
DESPERATE MEASURES

The next Monday, Pi leaned against her locker, feeling nauseated.

May 1st was coming up fast. She had until then to reply to Harvard. Harvard did not grant extensions. No extensions, no exceptions.

What if she turned Harvard down and then lost her ESP? Diamond wouldn't want her, and then where would she be?

Nowhere.

She hadn't felt this queasy since her SATs, when she'd consumed a gallon of coffee just to make sure she stayed alert. Which she had gotten a perfect score on, by the way.

Maybe she should accept. That had been her plan all along. Go to Harvard. Become a famous scientist. Win the Nobel Prize. Was she crazy for considering not going?

She'd been accepted around the same time that Diamond had recruited her. She'd also been accepted at twelve other colleges, but she'd turned them all down. It was either Harvard or Diamond. She wanted Diamond.

No, she decided. She was not crazy. The only reason she'd wanted to go to a great school in the first place was to land a killer job.

We laughed whenever she used the expression "killer job".

Do you think she'll actually kill people?

Only if you can bore someone to death.

True, science was her first love, but Diamond was bigger. It was a bigger life. An exceptional one.

She'd wanted to start right away, but her father had insisted she finish high school. At least she'd have that, in case she changed her mind and decided to go to college later on. Which, of course, was what he was hoping.

But what if she was in the middle of interrogating a terrorist, when bam, just like that, she couldn't hear his thoughts? The next thing you knew, she'd be packing her bags. Bye-bye big, important life.

Or maybe she'd lose it sooner. The way things were going, she'd probably lose it the moment she turned down Harvard.

Maybe she *shouldn't* turn them down. She could always back out later. All she would lose was the deposit.

Or she could defer.

Harvard wouldn't give extensions, but they did allow you to defer. They even encouraged it. Take a year off, travel. Work in a think tank. Sure, they meant real think tank and not pretend think tank and secret spy program. But anyway.

If she deferred, she would still have Harvard if she lost her ESP.

But what if Diamond found out? How could they *not* find out? They were a spy program! Collecting intelligence was their thing. They wouldn't want her if they thought she wasn't totally committed. She had only met the head of the program, Lawrence Stoddard, once in a boardroom in DC, and he did not seem like the kind of person to suffer fools. He'd worn sleek black sunglasses, a black suit, and an unreadable expression.

Stoddard would absolutely rescind her offer if he thought she was losing her ESP.

She slammed her locker shut and headed down the hallway. The only person in sight was her archenemy, Jon Matthews. Okay, maybe "enemy" was too strong a word. Rival was better. Or maybe, nemesis? He was the only other student who'd gotten a perfect score on the SATs. Plus, he was the class valedictorian.

He'd also gotten into Harvard. She'd wanted to be the only one from their school, but he'd ruined that for her, too.

Over the two and a half years since developing telepathy, she'd eavesdropped on him many times to try to understand what went through that brain of his. He was so relaxed it infuriated her. She had to study all the time to get the grades she did, while it just seemed to come to him so easily. He never even tried.

There goes honey Pi, he thought as she passed him in the

hallway. *We both know Harvard would never have accepted her if she didn't have ESP.*

She stopped in her tracks and stared at him. He stared back.

That's bullshit! she thought straight at him, even though she knew he couldn't hear. *And, seriously, did he just call me "honey Pi"?* She strode on, furious, leaving Matthews still staring after her. He could have it. Valedictorian. Harvard. The whole Ivy League, for all she cared. He could have it all. She had ESP, and she had Diamond.

And she intended to keep them both. She would figure it out. She had to. She was turning Harvard down.

The week went by quickly. No one else lost their ESP, and we all went back to our normal routines. Normal for us, that is.

Mackenzie was trying to come to terms with her mother's cancer. The surgery was scheduled for Thursday, and Mackenzie was all nerves. We felt terrible for her.

Tess and BJ were still having sex. A lot.

Cooper was still gambling and smoking.

Olivia was trying to not pick her nails. Or worry. Or panic.

Meanwhile, Pi spent night after night taking notes, doing research, and taking more notes. She would *not* lose her ESP. She would figure this out. But she was getting nowhere. All she knew was what the Centers for Disease Control and Prevention had told us: our condition was the result of a new preservative called NFG, which had been used to stabilize the flu vaccine.

It was late Sunday night when her phone pinged. She'd been reading up on the history of vaccinations. From smallpox to polio, measles to mumps, it was all fascinating. She reluctantly tore herself away from her reading and picked up her phone.

It was Nick:

```
Guys, I lost it.
```

Three down, and not a cure in sight.

* * *

"Let me get this straight," Jon said. "You're asking for *my* help?"

If someone had told Pi that one day she'd be standing across from Jon Matthews and asking for his help, she wouldn't have believed it. But desperate times called for desperate measures.

If anyone could help her, he could. Not because he was smarter, but because he had a different way of looking at things. At least, that's what she'd told herself as she entered the music room where he was playing his guitar.

He'd barely acknowledged her presence. He just sat there, strumming away, as if she were invisible. Six minutes later, he casually looked up from his guitar and said, "I take it you're not here because you're a fan of my music."

She flushed. She had to admit, he sounded pretty good. He looked good, too: the way he leaned into the guitar, his hair flopping into his eyes. And sexy. That is, if she were into that type. Which she wasn't. She didn't even have a type. She had a plan.

"I prefer the drums," she said stiffly, then felt her face redden. Seriously, drums? Who preferred drums?

He raised an eyebrow, then laughed. "I should have known you'd be into something more aggressive. So why the honor, honey Pi? Why are you here?"

She felt like walking out. He was so damn condescending. But, instead, she swallowed her pride and drew in a breath. "I need your help," she started, "but there's just one thing. You have to promise you won't tell anyone."

He looked amused. "That I'm helping you?" *She's kind of cute when she begs.*

Jerk. She shook her head. "No. It's about the Espies. But first you have to promise you won't say a word about what I'm going to tell you." This was high school. People talked. Rumors spread. Who knew how long it would be before Dr Dail heard something was up?

"And what do I get in return?" *She should smile. Why does she always look so miserable?*

The conversation was *making* her miserable. "The satisfaction of knowing that you might be saving the human race," she said.

He started tuning the guitar. "Ah. I presume this has something to do with the Espies losing their ESP. Precisely, Jordana and Anojah." He looked up at her. "Am I right?"

Pi's mouth dropped open. "How...how did you know that?"

"Because I'm not an idiot," he said. "I notice things. Like when I ran into Jordana in the media room and noticed that her eyes were normal." *Pi has interesting eyes. The purple tinge makes her look exotic.*

Pi felt like kicking herself. She'd never even considered the eye thing. None of us had. Fortunately, our teachers could barely see anything through their sunglasses and we rarely interacted with other kids. Still, perhaps she should insist that the ex-Espies wear colored contacts.

"And now there's another one down," she said, frowning. "Nick lost his, too."

"And you're afraid it'll happen to you," Jon said, tightening the bottom string. He plucked it a few times, then tightened it some more. "You're worried about Diamond."

"You know about Diamond, too?" Her eyes narrowed. "Are you spying on me?" Good Lord, was he stalking her? He couldn't really believe she'd be interested in him. Please! She wouldn't go out with him if he had the highest IQ in the world. She couldn't stand him.

"No," he said. "I just pay attention, *honey Pi*."

"Look, forget I asked," she said, and turned to leave. "I don't have time for this condescending bullshit. I'm on a tight schedule."

"Sit," he said, motioning to the chair next to his.

"Excuse me?"

"I said sit. Do you want to save humanity or what?" *She's so touchy.*

Sighing, she sat down.

"Fine," he said. "I'll help you."

"Why?" she asked suspiciously. She tried to read his mind, but all she got was, *This is fun.*

He resumed his strumming. "Now, start at the beginning. Tell me what you know, and I'll figure out the rest."

Chapter Fourteen

IS THERE A DOCTOR IN THE HOUSE?

"I have a plan," Pi said the next morning in the school cafeteria. Instead of texting, she'd called each and every one of us at 5 a.m. to make sure we all showed up. It went something like this:

Pi: Hi. It's me. Emergency meeting
in the cafeteria. 7:00 a.m. sharp. Be there.
Dave: Who *is* this?
Olivia: It's 5 in the morning! Is someone hurt?
Sadie: Are you crazy? It's 5 a.m.! You woke up Dumbo!
I mean Michael!
Cooper: Hmmmn?
Daniel: Who *is* this?

We were now sitting at one of the tables, trying not to fall asleep. "Let me begin by thanking you all for coming," Pi said, smiling. "I appreciate it."

Why is she being so nice?

It couldn't wait till after breakfast?

This is a cafeteria, idiot. Have some oatmeal.

"So what's the plan?" Isaac asked.

Pi cleared her throat. "For starters, I'm dividing you into groups."

Why is she always so bossy?

I need a nap.

"We already have assigned lab groups," Mona pointed out, making eyes at Mars. "If we're getting reorganized, can I still be with Mars?"

He blew her a kiss.

"This isn't Lab," Pi said. "We're not playing games. These are scientific control groups. I've come up with a plan to stop our telepathy from disappearing." *Actually, it was Jon who came up with it. But I did all the work.*

Jon Matthews?

You told him about our problem? You weren't supposed to tell anyone!

"I admit it," she said. "I told him. But we're desperate. I figured two heads were better than one." *Especially two brilliant heads, even though his is stuck up his butt.*

Like yours isn't?

I can't believe the great and powerful Pi asked someone for help. Alert the media!

Pi gritted her teeth. She didn't need this crap. It had been embarrassing enough running to the class valedictorian for help. She sighed inwardly. At least it had paid off.

Yesterday in the music room, she'd explained the problem to Jon in detail, starting with what she knew about NFG, the mysterious compound in the flu shots, and ending with Nick losing his ESP. Jon had told Pi he was going home to do some research and would call her as soon as he found anything out.

Two hours later, her phone rang.

"You need a booster," he said.

"We already thought of that. But we don't even know if the compound still exists. And even if it does, how are we supposed to get a hold of it?"

"I'm not talking about the compound," he said. "I'm talking about supplements. There are seventeen of you left, right? That means the NFG is still in your system. You don't have to replace it, just boost it."

"And just how do you know this, Sherlock?"

"Apparently, around the same time NFG was used in your flu vaccination, a similar compound was used on an experimental vineyard in California."

"As a preservative?"

"That was the idea. Prior to implantation, the grape seeds were treated with TFG."

"TFG."

"Yes.

"Did it work?"

"Oh, it was literally a huge success – the grapes mutated to the size of melons."

"That's not what a preservative does. A preservative preserves."

"No kidding. But that's what happened. And let me tell you, they were *thrilled* with their discovery. They made millions."

"So how does this information help me?"

"After about one year, some of the vines went back to producing normal-size fruit. Tests showed that the TFG was wearing off. They tried boosting it by applying massive amounts of fertilizer, and it worked – but only on the vines that still had traces of it left. On these, the melon-grapes continued to flourish."

"How did you find this out?" Pi asked. She'd spent days researching and had never found any of this.

"It's all password protected. I did some hacking."

Pi was impressed, though she'd never admit it. "So you think our contaminated NFG was actually TFG?"

"Possibly. Or something like it. That's beside the point."

"And the point is we need to find our own nutrient?"

He nodded. "Something that nourishes the body the way fertilizer nourishes the soil."

"Supplements, vitamins – that sort of thing?"

"Something to energize the NFG."

"Or TFG."

"Right. Bottom line, it can be saved, as long as there's still some left in your system."

"Okay," Pi said. "Can you recommend supplements?"

"Don't get lazy on me, Pi. I said I'd help you, not do everything. Just keep in mind that it's the NFG with the power. The supplements just boost it, so don't look for anything too esoteric. The fertilizer is a case in point. It wasn't anything special."

After they hung up, Pi had made a large pot of coffee and spent the night Googling viable supplements. With any luck, at least one of them would revitalize the compound that was still in our system.

"How exactly will this plan work?" Levi asked now. "I didn't understand anything you were thinking."

No surprise there, Pi thought. "We're going to stimulate the NFG," she replied.

"Sounds sexy," BJ said.

Daniel perked up. "Sex is involved?"

"There is no sex involved," Pi said wearily.

No plan of Pi's would involve sex.

What about that Oxford guy?

What about Jon? It's obvious he wants a piece of his honey Pi.

Pi felt her cheeks grow hot. "Enough!" she ordered and stood up beside the table. "Here's how it's going to work. There will be six groups. Groups 1 and 2 will focus on hearing, since hearing is how we perceive people's thoughts. Groups 3 and 4 will focus on sight, since it's through the eyes that the thoughts are transmitted. The last two groups are for the brain, since the brain controls everything. I picked out six different supplements, one per group. It is my hope that some of them will be successful in saving our ESP. Best-case scenario: they all work. Worst-case scenario: none of them work. You are to stop at a pharmacy today and pick up your supplement. The sooner you get started, the better your chances. You will take your medicine faithfully."

"There aren't going to be injections, are there?" Mackenzie asked, looking worried. She really, really, hated needles.

A hot beef injection? BJ thought with a straight face.

We groaned.

What does that even mean?

It's from The Breakfast Club. *Don't you have Netflix?*

"No, Mackenzie," Pi said, ignoring the rest of us. "You can take them orally."

BJ smirked. *I do like oral…*

We groaned again. Tess elbowed him in the stomach and groaned the loudest.

"I thought we weren't supposed to take any drugs," Mona said. "What about the interactions? Exactly what will we be taking?"

"We were warned against taking pharmaceuticals," Pi explained. "These are just supplements. I've narrowed it down to ginkgo, magnesium, lutein, zeaxanthin, DHA, and cognizin citicoline. They're over-the-counter supplements shown to increase eye, ear, and cognitive function. Some of them have other uses, too – not just what I've assigned them for. Like ginkgo, for instance. I put it in one of the ears groups because it's used to treat sudden hearing loss. But it's also good for eye problems and memory disorders."

Hey, Edward, Levi thought, looking at his iPhone. *You*

should be in that group. It says here it's also used for sexual disorders.

That happened once!

We all started Googling.

"Why is lutein on the list?" Tess asked. "It says that people taking it have reported hearing loss."

"In my opinion—" Brinn started, but was interrupted by Pi.

"Yes, I read that, too," she said. "But it only happened to people with osteoporosis, high blood pressure, arthritis, high cholesterol, and depression. It's great for preventing eye disease, so unless anyone has any of these conditions, lutein stays on the list."

"Why the groups?" Sadie asked, gesturing around the cafeteria. "Why can't we all take everything?"

Pi frowned. "Because your brain might fry at the dosage I'm prescribing."

Prescribing? So now she's a doctor?

"I want to take them all!" Courtney exclaimed. "I don't want to lose my ESP!"

It's not like it could hurt her, Levi thought. *Her brain is already fried.*

Pi shook her head. "You can't take them all. It would be way too dangerous, as in low blood pressure dangerous. As in not getting enough oxygen to your brain and going into shock. Not to mention nausea and diarrhea."

Ew.

I'd rather have ESP with diarrhea than no ESP with no diarrhea.

Can we please change the subject?

"We all want to take what works," Tess said.

"But that's the point," Pi said. "We don't know what works. That's why it's an experiment. This way we can see what works and what doesn't. We'll know when something doesn't work when someone loses their telepathy."

Levi clenched his jaw. "This is a terrible plan. What if only one supplement works? Only a few of us will be saved."

"No," Pi said. "Even if just one works, most of us will be saved. As soon as someone in a group becomes thought-deaf, the rest of the group starts taking something else. So, in theory, only five people – one from each of the other groups – will lose their ESP."

"But how do we know if it's the supplement or if we just didn't take a high enough dosage?" Sadie asked.

"That's why we're taking *really* high doses," Pi explained. *What is wrong with these people? Are they not listening?*

"So that's it, then," Michelle said. "We're your guinea pigs."

"We're *our* guinea pigs," Pi responded. "Any more questions?"

"Isn't DHA in tuna?" Sadie asked, looking up from her phone.

"Yes," Pi said. "Why do you ask?"

"Because I eat tuna all the time!"

"Then maybe that's why you still have ESP," Olivia said. "Did Nick eat fish?"

We all looked around. Nick wasn't there. Neither was Cooper.

"This meeting was mandatory," Pi said, sounding annoyed.

"Did I not make myself clear on the phone?"

Bossy, bossy, bossy!

I hope Cooper's okay, Mackenzie thought.

Olivia stiffened. *He's fine, Mackenzie. He's just tired.*

Is that code for hungover? Isaac thought.

"Nick just texted me," Mars said. "He decided not to come. He says, and I quote, 'I'm over it.'"

Over it?

OVER IT?

It's only been two days!

He should still come to these meetings.

You think he still wants to come to these meetings? I didn't even want to come. It's seven o'clock in the freaking morning!

"If Nick doesn't have to come," Anojah said, "neither should I."

"I have a question," Jordana said. "You said that this plan might prevent some of you from losing your ESP. But can it bring mine back?" *Is my NFG totally defunct?*

"It...um..."

"Crap," Jordana said.

"I have a question, too," Anojah said. "If this plan can't help us, why the hell did you wake us up at five in the morning?"

"Which reminds me," Pi continued, completely ignoring her, "I hereby make it mandatory for those who've lost their ESP to wear purple contacts."

"You're not the boss of me," Anojah snapped. "What do I care if people know I've lost it?"

Pi glared at her. "Do you really want to be the person who

lets the cat out of the bag and ruins it for the rest of us?"

Anojah stood up. "Fine. Whatever. But I'm outta here."

Jordana looked like she was going to be sick. "If you guys don't mind, I'd like to stay. Maybe Pi is wrong. Maybe one of these supplements will bring it back."

There's absolutely no chance it will bring it back. "No problem," Pi said brightly. "So I guess that makes eighteen of us. Three per group. An even split."

"I want to be in Pi's group," Courtney announced.

"Why?" Tess asked.

"Because she's going to take the best supplement herself."

The rest of us wanted to be in her group, too.

Pi flushed. "What makes you think I know which supplement will work? Don't you think you'd know if I knew?"

Good point, Sadie thought.

"So how do we decide who gets what?" Mona asked.

"We should pick our groups out of a hat," Olivia said. "That way, no one gets shafted."

"Fine," Pi said. "I'll write out all the options and we can cut them up and put them in the hat. Does anyone have scissors?"

"I do!" Jordana sang, reaching for her manicure set.

"I'll pick for Cooper," Olivia said.

"Can you get him to stop smoking?" Pi asked. "It might interfere with the supplements."

"I can't promise that, no."

Pi sighed. "Who has a hat?"

No one responded.

"Fine, then. Does anyone have a bowl?"

Like a bong bowl?

"No," Pi said, rolling her eyes. "Like a cereal bowl."

Why would anyone have a cereal bowl? Sadie thought.

Hello? thought Pi. *We're in a cafeteria!*

"I'll get one," Olivia offered, and came back a minute later with a paper one.

"Okay, guys," Pi said, and put down the scissors. "I'm ready. There are eighteen pieces of paper. On each piece is a group number, along with the name of a supplement and its corresponding category." She put them in the paper bowl, covered it with her hand and shook it all up.

We picked.

Gingko is one of the good ones, right? I got Group 2.

Me, too!

I got a Brain. Yay!

Pi had Eyes. She was with Sadie and Jordana in Group 4. *Things could be worse*, she thought. *I could be with Levi.*

I heard that.

"I have to switch groups," Mackenzie announced. "I have to take magnesium."

"Sorry," Pi said. "No switching. Why should one person get a preference and not another?"

"Because I'm already taking it and I'm not allowed to stop. I have a deficiency."

Pi sighed. "Mackenzie, why didn't you mention this before?"

"I forgot?"

"Fine," Pi grumbled. "Does anyone in Ears 1 want to switch with Mackenzie? She's in Brain 6."

"I will," Courtney offered.

Good move, Courtney. You need all the brain power you can get.

"I want to be with Mona," Mars said. "BJ got to be with Tess, and even the twins are together."

"If Mars changes groups, then I want to be with Cooper," Olivia declared.

"Enough!" Pi said. "This isn't musical chairs. Mackenzie switches with Courtney, and the rest of you stay put. Can we please continue?"

There was a chorus of fines, all rights, and whatevers.

Pi took out her iPad. "When I call your name, give me your group number and I'll put you on the spreadsheet."

After everyone was accounted for, this is what she had:

Group 1 EARS	Group 2 EARS	Group 3 EYES	Group 4 EYES	Group 5 BRAIN	Group 6 BRAIN
Magnesium	Gingko	Lutein	Zeaxanthin	DHA	Cognizin citicoline
Mackenzie	Cooper	Isaac	Pi	Tess	Michelle
Brinn	Daniel	Olivia	Sadie	BJ	Courtney
Edward	Dave	Mona	*Jordana (no ESP)	Mars	Levi

"Just one more thing," she said. "In addition to these supplements, I suggest you start taking some resveratrol. It's the only substance that will be common to all of us. It probably won't stimulate the NFG, but it will help boost our immune systems. It's also good for the heart."

"What's resveratrol?" Dave asked.

"It's a polyphenol compound found in red wine."

Daniel perked up. "Are you saying we should drink wine?"

"Yes," Pi said. "As long as it's red."

We all cheered.

Chapter Fifteen
IF THE SHOES FIT...

"Thanks for coming out to dinner," Mackenzie said, taking a spoonful of soup. "I missed you."

Tess felt guilty. Now that she and BJ were, well, *closer*, she hadn't had much time for Mackenzie. *I'm a terrible best friend.*

No, you're not. You're in a love haze. And I've been busy, too. But I'm happy to see you.

It was Thursday evening, two days after we started taking the supplements, and no one else had lost their telepathy. Mackenzie and Tess were having dinner at Bite. With fairy lights strung across the ceiling and little trinkets everywhere, Bite was Mackenzie's favorite restaurant in Tribeca. The walls were decorated with colorful murals, and in the corner was a stone fireplace, closed for the coming summer.

"Where did you get that shirt?" Tess asked, motioning to the patchy green V-neck Mackenzie was wearing. "I love it."

"It's an old shirt," she said. "It had food stains on it and I was going to toss it but then I thought…maybe I could cut the stains out and fill them in with another shirt I had."

"You know how to sew?" Tess asked.

"Yeah," Mackenzie said. "Don't you?"

Tess laughed. "No! You're like a designer!"

"Hah!"

"No, seriously. You could be the next Diane von Furstenberg."

"Yeah, right. I cut out stains. I was just…trying to keep busy." She'd wanted to flip through magazines with her mom, like they always did, or talk, but her mother had wanted to watch soaps. Alone. So Mackenzie had decided to clean out her closet.

"Wait," Tess said. "Wasn't her surgery today?"

Mackenzie sighed. "She has the flu. They have to reschedule."

The flu? In April?

I know! Crazy, huh?

On top of cancer?

They both shook their heads.

I just hope the cancer doesn't spread while we're waiting. Mackenzie imagined the cancer like ink stains on a shirt, slowly seeping through the material, turning it black. She wished she could just cut those stains out, too. Replace them with something else.

"I'm sure the doctors know what they're doing," Tess said.

"And I'm glad *you* have a new hobby."

Cleaning out my closet?

Making shirts.

I wanted to spend time with my mom. But she doesn't want me there.

"Of course she does," Tess said. "She's your mom."

Mackenzie frowned.

"Move over?" she'd asked her mother the other day, trying to climb into bed with her.

"Don't, Mackie," her mother had said. "I don't want you to get sick."

She has the flu! Tess thought. *She doesn't want to get you sick!*

That's not it. She doesn't want me to hear her thoughts. Even more than usual. She's avoiding me. When I got home yesterday, I went to her room to say goodnight, but she was wearing an eye mask.

"Maybe she was asleep?" *She loves you. She just wants to protect you.*

I don't need to be protected! She's my mother! I'm not going to break into a thousand pieces at the word "cancer"! I can't believe they hid out in a hotel! They won't tell me anything! My mom won't let me near her! Like I can't Google "cancer" and come up with a million scary scenarios on my own?

"Maybe she just wants some privacy," Tess offered. "She needs to process it all, you know?"

"Maybe."

"She just needs her space."

Mackenzie shook her head and picked up her sandwich.

She took a massive bite. "How's the love den?" she asked, her mouth full of grilled cheese.

Tess beamed. "Great. I have no complaints."

She looks happy, Mackenzie thought. *She's in love.* She barely remembered the feeling. After she and Cooper broke up, she'd had a few boyfriends, but it was never the same. None of them had lasted more than a month.

Cooper was a million years ago, Tess thought, reading her mind.

So were you and BJ, and you're still together.

Tess was quiet for a moment. Then she said, "Do you want him back?"

No. That ship has sailed.

Not if he's picturing you in the shower…

Mackenzie waved her hand. *Olivia was making a big deal out of nothing. All guys picture us in the shower.* She took another bite of grilled cheese. *But it would be nice to have a BJ.*

Tess winked. *BJ said the same thing to me last night.*

Mackenzie snorted.

Tess reached into her purse and took out a small bottle. "I have to take these with food," she said, struggling with the top. "Am I the only one who has issues with the childproofing?"

"Yes," Mackenzie said. "Do you want me to do it?"

"No, I got it." It snapped open, and Tess shook out two massive pills. "Bottoms up. I take the rest at bedtime with a cookie and a glass of milk."

"Do you really think this is going to work?" Mackenzie asked.

"It seems to be working so far. At least, it's not *not* working."

"What group are you in again?" Mackenzie asked, finishing off her sandwich.

"Brain 5, DHA. I'm with BJ and Mars. What about you? You're with Edward and Brinn, right?"

Mackenzie made a face. "That girl stinks like bananas."

"That's because she's always eating them. She must be seriously constipated," Tess said.

"Why?"

"Bananas are constipating! I wasn't allowed to eat them as a kid because then I'd only poop, like, once a week." *Sorry. Poop is not appropriate dinner conversation.*

I'd rather talk about poop than cancer.

Tess laughed.

"What are you doing this weekend?" Mackenzie asked, with a smile.

"Teddy's having a party. His parents are going away. Wanna come?"

Teddy Barboza and Tess used to be best friends. Actually, Tess was in love with him before she was in love with BJ, but he hadn't felt the same way. These days he spent most of his time at wrestling matches. He and Tess had stayed friends, not best friends, but friendly enough that she was still invited to his parties.

"I don't know," Mackenzie said. "I don't feel much like partying." On the other hand, she didn't feel like spending a Saturday night in her room, being shut out by her mother.

Tess wasn't sure she wanted to go, either. She'd rather just lock herself in her love den. But parties were fun, too.

The waitress came back to their table with menus. "Would you ladies care for dessert?"

I'm stuffed, Tess thought.

I don't want to go back, Mackenzie thought. *Not yet.*

Tess smiled up at her waitress. "Sure," she said. "We'll take a look."

It was after ten when Mackenzie approached her building. She was about to step through the revolving door when Bennett walked out. Bennett D'Attilo, the hot private school guy who used to live five floors above her.

Bennett D'Attilo, the guy she'd cheated on Cooper with.

Except he no longer went to private school and he no longer lived at home. He was a year older and had already graduated. He'd rented an apartment in Williamsburg and was studying film at NYU.

She hadn't seen him in months. In fact, she could count on one hand the number of times she'd run into him these past couple of years. When he was in high school, they'd had different schedules, and now that he was in college, he hardly ever came home.

"Hey, stranger," he said. "How've you been?"

"Fine," she said curtly.

He reached into his pocket and pulled out a joint. "Want to go for a walk?"

"Thanks but no thanks," she said.

He smiled. "I know something else we could do."

"What's that?"

He laughed. "What, you don't know? Some mind reader you are."

She read what was on his mind, and blood rushed to her face. "I'm not going up to the terrace with you," she said, rolling her eyes. The terrace was on the eighth floor. It was where they used to hook up when she was a freshman.

"This mind reading thing is freaky. I like it." *Less talking, more action.*

"Goodbye, Bennett," she said, turning away. "It's been fun."

"Wait," he said, reaching for her wrist. "What about a party?"

"What, now?" She broke free of his hold. "I'm late, Bennett. I have to—"

"Saturday. In Brooklyn. Come with me. Meet my friends."

That would be a first. When they were together, he'd never take her anywhere, let alone introduce her to his friends. All he'd wanted to do was hook up, get high, and hook up some more.

Then she got it. She was semi-famous now, and it stroked his ego to be seen with her. She almost laughed. The super-cool private-school guy had turned into a groupie.

"Come on," he said. "Say yes. You know you want to."

"So now you're a mind reader, too?"

She had to admit, she was tempted. So what if he was a groupie? She still felt wanted. She thought about her situation at home. Feeling wanted was a lot more appealing than feeling shut out.

She knew she should say no. She'd told Tess she didn't feel like partying, and it was true. She'd just be a downer. Besides, her mother needed her at home.

Didn't she?

Not really. She didn't even want her there. Her mother needed her space.

She turned back to Bennett. "Sure, why not?"

The next day during lunch, Mackenzie was in the bathroom, debating whether to cancel on Bennett. It was all she could think about, and the bathroom was always the perfect place for important decisions. Even though there was some open space underneath the partition, the wall prevented anyone from hearing her thoughts:

He was a jerk last time. Why won't he be a jerk this time? This time I don't really care. It's just one night. It's not a big deal.

Could you please stop?

Wait. What?

That last thought hadn't been hers.

Was someone listening to her?

It sounded like Michelle. But how could it be Michelle? Michelle couldn't hear through walls. No one could.

Except Mackenzie.

I'm imagining it, she thought. *What else could it be?*

Her conscience?

Maybe going to a party with Bennett wasn't a good idea. Bennett was the reason she'd broken up with Cooper. If Cooper found out, it would be like a slap in the face. And of course he'd find out.

He already knew she was thinking about it. We all did. *Is she serious?* he'd thought that morning in homeroom. *That guy's so sleazy.*

But he's hot! Courtney thought.

Who's Bennett? Mona wondered.

Why does Cooper even care? Olivia wondered, picking her nails. Pick. Pick. Pick.

I'm just looking out for her!

Cooper didn't want her back. Why would he? She had cheated on him. She'd loved him, but she'd been a bad girlfriend.

He was just worried about her.

She was worried about herself, too.

Oh my god, get over yourself. It's just a stupid party. Go.

What the hell? Who *was* that?

She couldn't make out the voice in her head. Yet it sounded familiar. It seemed to be coming from the stall next to hers.

Straining her neck, she peeked under the partition. She noticed the shoes immediately. They were bright white sneakers.

Brinn's shoes.

You can hear me? Mackenzie thought.

"Apparently," Brinn said.

The supplements had begun to kick in, although not in the way we'd envisioned. We didn't know it then, but our powers were growing.

Brinn could now hear through walls.

Chapter Sixteen
TOMMY CAN YOU HEAR ME?

"I can't believe you made me come to a video arcade."

"This is a pinball parlor," Jon said, a little indignantly. "And not just any pinball parlor. This is Pauline's, the most famous pinball parlor in Times Square, maybe even the country. This is *history*. Did you know that pinball dates back to at least the fifteenth century? It comes from games like bowling and croquet."

No, Pi didn't know. Nor did she care. She grimaced. Lining the walls was one hideous machine after another. Some had cartoon characters, others had stars and banners. Plus, they were really loud.

"This isn't history," she said. "This is tacky. Tell me, what's so important that I had to ruin a perfectly good Saturday afternoon and meet you in this hellhole?"

"No one forced you," he replied.

"It's not like I had a choice."

After the bathroom incident on Friday, all the Espies went bonkers.

Is it a fluke? Can Brinn really hear through walls?

I don't know, Pi thought back.

Is it because of the supplements? Does this mean they're working?

I don't know!

I already hear through walls, thought Mackenzie. *What does that mean?*

I don't know!

So call Jon! We need to know what's going on.

Pi sighed. She didn't want to call him, but what else could she do?

She'd texted him after school. He wrote back immediately saying he had some ideas, and that she should meet him the next day at 2 p.m. in Times Square.

Here, at the arcade. Correction: parlor.

Seriously, pinball? Was he ten? She didn't want to go. She didn't want to meet him anywhere, for that matter. And why Times Square? Was he a tourist?

She could have texted him back that she was busy. She could have asked him to email his ideas. But she didn't.

We had plenty to think about that.

"Brinn is being enhanced," he was saying now. He inserted a token at the side of a machine, then looked back at Pi. "Her supplement is stimulating the NFG. It's magnesium, right? The rest of her group will probably start hearing through walls, too."

"Mackenzie already can," Pi said, and a light went on in her head. "Wow. I can't believe I didn't make that connection before. It *is* the magnesium. Mackenzie was taking it even before we started the experiment."

Ugh. Pi wished she'd been in that group.

"Are those of us taking other supplements going to be enhanced in some way, too?" she asked.

Jon shrugged. "Beats me." He pressed a button on the side of the machine. "You want to go first?"

"No, I don't want to go first. I don't want to go at all! I want to hear your ideas. You said you had ideas."

"That's all I got."

"You dragged me all the way to this tourist trap for that?"

He laughed. "I thought you'd like it. It's fun."

She was about make a snarky remark when the machine came to life and bells sounded everywhere. "I take it you don't like *Tommy*," he said over the din.

Three silver balls rolled into a track on the right of the machine. He pulled on a rod, and the first ball went shooting into the playfield. Suddenly the machine went into a frenzy. *Zing! Bang! Ka-chink!* She didn't think it was possible, but more lights lit up, and it got even noisier. Everything was whirling and spinning like fireworks on the Fourth of July.

"What's happening?" In spite of herself, Pi was intrigued. It was a fascinating machine, for an antique.

"I just scored 10,000 points," Jon said, all excited. His hair fell over his eyes, and she had to admit he looked kind of cute. He continued to bat the ball from target to target until, finally, his aim failed and the ball rolled down the drain. When he pulled on the rod for the next ball, his arm brushed against hers, giving her a charge.

She told herself it was static electricity. "So who's Tommy?" she asked, suddenly aware of Jon's body next to hers. He was standing so close she could smell his cologne.

A lot of cologne.

Did he like her? Yes. She was pretty sure he liked her.

"Tell me you're kidding," he said, flipping the ball from target to target, accumulating points with each pop and whir. "You need to get out more. It's the most famous rock opera of all time. You at least know the song, 'Tommy Can You Hear Me,' don't you? The Who?"

"Who?" she asked.

"They were only one of the most influential rock bands of the twentieth century." *Wow. She really does live under a rock.*

"Tell me about Tommy," she said. "Since I've been living under a rock and all."

"It's a cool story," he said, his eyes never leaving the playfield. "Tommy's mother brainwashes him into believing he can't see or hear anything, so he learns to rely on his sense of touch and imagination and becomes a pinball expert."

"Does he ever get to see or hear again?"

Thwack! Ding, ding! Clang! Five thousand more points lit up the scoreboard.

"Yeah!" Jon cheered, his eyes shining. Pi also noticed his smile. It was wide and contagious. She found herself smiling, too.

"Yeah, but much later," he replied, batting away with the flippers. He missed and, like its predecessor, the ball went down the drain. "His mother smashes a mirror, and it removes his mental block."

Breaking a mirror brought back your senses? Who knew? Maybe she should try it on the Espies who'd lost their ESP.

Everything went quiet.

"What happened?" she asked. "Did you break the machine?"

He laughed. "Nope. I'm out. Which means you're up. Now you get to beat my score."

"Piece of cake," she said, with more confidence than she felt. There was more to this than she'd originally thought. Like when to hit the flippers and how far to pull the rod. Or how to nudge the machine without alerting the sensors. Or how to refrain from punching out the coin door in utter frustration.

Clang! Slam! Thump! Ka-chink!

Two hours later, Jon was behind by 250 points. "Not bad for a rookie," he said. "You're a fast learner, honey Pi. What do you say we call it a draw and get some coffee?"

"No way," she said, pressing the start button. "I intend to kick your ass."

Later, sitting across from each other at a coffee place called Flat White, he shook his head and said, "I can't believe you beat me."

She laughed. "You created a monster."

"I should call you Frankenstein."

"Frankenstein was the scientist," Pi corrected, "not the monster. I'd have to call *you* Frankenstein."

"Have you always been such a know-it-all?"

She smiled. "Yes," she said. "You?"

"You know it," he answered.

This time they both laughed, and at the same time.

"I had fun," he said, sipping his coffee. *She has a cute laugh.* "Of course, we both know I would have won if you hadn't been so…distracting." *She's kinda sexy.*

She'd been called a lot of things in her life – brilliant, bossy, even bitchy – but never sexy. She wasn't sure how to process this.

Oh, yeah, he definitely liked her. But he liked a lot of girls. He was always dating someone, wasn't he?

He leaned forward, and for a moment she thought he was going to kiss her, right there in the coffee shop. But instead, he reached across the table for more sugar and then stirred it into his cup. "I like my coffee really sweet," he said, and she let herself breathe.

She did not want him to kiss her. Did she?

She gave him a flirty smile.

He smiled back.

She had to admit, it was nice being around someone who was her equal.

Almost her equal, she amended.

"How many girlfriends have you had?" she blurted.

He grinned. "Should I make a list?"

"How many *serious* girlfriends?"

"A few," he answered, after a pause. "I like having a girlfriend."

"But you're single now."

"Yes."

"What happened to your last one?"

"We weren't a good match."

"Why not?"

He cocked his head to the side. "She thought Europe was a country."

Hah. "So you like airheads?"

"They do seem to be my type," he admitted.

"I have someone to fix you up with," she said. "Do you know Jordana? You guys would get along great."

"I'm trying to get out of the airhead business." He looked meaningfully at her. "What about you? Why don't you have a boyfriend?"

Pi wasn't much for relationships. She'd hooked up with an Oxford student working in Manhattan for the summer this past August. She'd wanted to see what the all fuss was about, and he'd seemed interested. He was also curious about her ESP, since he'd heard about us in the news. Besides all that, he'd genuinely found her attractive and she'd found him attractive and so they did it. Her first kiss, first everything. She'd approached it clinically and methodically, the way she did everything. Then he went back to England, and she never looked back.

Of course, when the news leaked, we all freaked out.

I can't believe Pi had sex before I did! thought just about everyone who hadn't had sex.

"I'm a solitary kind of person," she said to Jon.

"You certainly are, honey Pi. You're a bit of a mystery. I wish I could read *your* mind."

"Could you not call me that?"

"What?"

"Honey Pi. It makes my skin crawl."

"Not honey Pi, not Frankenstein. What about Polly? Can I call you that? That's your real name, isn't it?" *I like it.*

"Please don't." Her mother called her Polly. When she bothered to call her anything.

"Tell me what you're thinking," he said, leaning closer. *I want to know her.*

She stared at him. "My mother calls me Polly, and I hate it. I hate her a little, too."

"Your mom… You don't live with her, right?"

"Nope," Pi said. "She lives in Indiana. She ditched me and my dad and remarried."

"Ouch," Jon said, his expression compassionate.

"I was eight when she left. I've had plenty of time to get over it." She forced a smile. Now he knew something about her, too. "Look, just call me Pi, okay? Everyone else does."

He nodded. "Okay, Pi it is."

"Okay then." She took a sip of her latte. "So," she said, "does Harvard have any pinball clubs? Or are you planning to try out for something more Ivy League, like water polo or lacrosse?"

"I'm not going to Harvard. Not yet, anyway. I decided to defer."

"Really? You did?" She put down her cup. "I'm not going either. But I didn't defer. I turned them down."

"Yeah, I heard." He gave her a look.

"What?" she asked.

"Nothing. I was just surprised. Ever since freshman year, all you ever talked about was going to Harvard."

"Well, something better came up. Opportunity knocked." She knew he knew she was going to work for Diamond, but he wouldn't know what it was. "What about you? What are your plans?"

He broke into a grin. "I'm backpacking around Australia."

Pi gaped at him. "You're not serious."

"I am," Jon said, his eyes lighting up. "I want to travel and see the world before starting school. I need a break."

"Take the summer off! Don't throw away a whole year!" She shook her head. "You're just going to find yourself another airhead. An Australian airhead. You should go to Harvard. You're being dumb."

"Like becoming a spy isn't dumb?"

He knew she was becoming a spy? "How do you know that?" she whispered.

"Because I'm *not* dumb. You Espies aren't that great at being sneaky. What kind of life are you going to have as a spy?"

"An exciting life," she said defensively. "A life that matters."

"What about fun?" he asked. "How does that fit into your master plan?"

"What makes you think your idea of fun is my idea of fun?"

"You liked pinball, didn't you? Maybe you should come

with me to Australia." *I can just picture her in a wetsuit, diving off the Great Barrier Reef.*

She blinked. He had to be joking. She tried to read his mind again, but all she got were fins and snorkels.

Oh, yeah, he liked her. He definitely liked her.

"My future," she announced, "does not include a wetsuit."

"Ouch," he said. "I get it. We obviously have different priorities."

He had that right. Very soon, she'd be on the fast track and he'd be traipsing though Australia, cavorting with backpackers and sheep. Bottom line, she had no intention of wasting a year of her life, and she certainly didn't want a boyfriend.

One day, maybe, she'd have time for a relationship, but when she did, it would be with someone more suited to her profession and character – another agent, perhaps, or a president of a small country. *Definitely not someone who'd choose sheep over Harvard.*

Back downtown, Mona was sitting next to Mars in the back row of the Union Square movie theater. They were watching some lame movie about zombie gorillas, and even though he had his hand up her skirt, she let her mind wander. It wasn't fair. Why should Tess and BJ be in the same group when she couldn't be with Mars? First thing Monday morning, she was going to talk to Pi. No matter what Bossy-Pants said, Mona was going to switch.

Definitely not someone who'd choose sheep over Harvard, a voice rang out in her head.

Huh?

She looked around to see who had thought that. But except for an old couple in the front row, they were alone in the theater.

And the voice wasn't coming from the old people. It sounded like Pi.

Who wasn't here. Was she?

Why are you thinking about Pi? Mars asked.

I don't know, Mona thought.

I need to get out of here, Pi's voice blabbed in her head.

Mona stood up and looked around the theater "Pi? Pi, are you here? Pi!"

The old people turned around and shushed her. Mona sat back down. *Something weird is going on.* She took out her phone and texted Pi.

```
Mona: Are you in the Union Square
movie theater?
Pi: No. Times Square.
Mona: Were you just thinking about
sheep?
Pi: How did you know that?
Mona: I heard you!
```

Mona stared at her phone.

Across town, Pi stared at her phone.

Her ESP is stronger, Pi thought. *First Brinn gets enhanced, now Mona. And let's not forget about Mackenzie. This is no coincidence. This is because of the supplements.*

I'm enhanced? Mona thought back, but then realized that Pi couldn't hear her back.

"You're the best, babe," Mars said, and Mona rolled her eyes. She focused back on Pi and, sure enough, Pi's thoughts zoned in again, loud and clear:

I have to call an emergency meeting. We should meet tonight.

Mona texted back:

```
Forget it. Tonight is date night.
```

Unlike some people she knew, namely Pi, Mona had a life. An enhanced life, apparently.

Chapter Seventeen
PARTY ANIMALS

Bennett showed up on a Harley.

Yes. The private-school preppy boy who summered in the Hamptons now had a Harley.

Mackenzie would have made fun of him, if she hadn't been secretly thrilled.

A Harley?

A Harley!

She'd never ever been on a motorcycle.

She put on the helmet he'd brought her, and climbed on behind him.

As they took turned onto the highway, she took in everything around her, down to the potholes in the road. The smell of his leather jacket. The wind at the back of her neck. The noise of the city whizzing by. She was hanging on to Bennett's waist, her blood rushing though her veins.

She was hanging on for dear life, and it thrilled her.

It was too loud to hear his thoughts. It was too loud to hear anyone's thoughts. It was too loud to think.

This was exactly what she needed. Who knew?

Fifteen minutes later, they pulled into the lot of a convenience store just across the bridge. "I need gas," he explained. Then: "Damn," he said, after filling up. "It's not taking my card. I have to pay inside. Be right back."

"I'm staying here," she said, still euphoric from the ride. She gazed up at the sky. She couldn't remember the last time she'd seen such a bright moon, but there it was, shining over Brooklyn.

She was enjoying a deep, cool breath when suddenly she heard Bennett's voice, right through the convenience store wall. Which was impossible, considering she was at least fifty feet away.

What was going on? Was her power growing?

She has a great ass, Mackenzie heard. *Love the pants. Girls should always wear leather.*

Who was he thinking about? Mackenzie wasn't wearing leather pants.

Was he flirting with someone? She looked around the lot. There wasn't a car in sight, which meant there were no other customers inside. Maybe the cashier?

Mackenzie sighed. He'd always been a flirt. Did she really think he'd changed?

She's funny, too. Too bad she's old enough to be my mother.

Okay, so he wasn't flirting. But still.

Maybe going to this party is a bad idea, he was thinking now. *Ella could be there. I think I was supposed to call her. Yeah, I was definitely supposed to call her.*

Did Mackenzie care that he was thinking about other girls?

No, she decided. She didn't. She just wanted to keep moving. She wanted to feel alive. She wanted to live in the moment.

"Hey," Bennett said, when he came out. "Ready to roll?"

"Do you mind if we skip the party?" she asked. "And just drive around?"

"I knew you'd like it," he said, as he climbed back on. He turned the key and the engine roared. "Where do you want to go?"

"Anywhere," she said, rewrapping her arms around him. "As long as we're moving."

She knew she could never trust him. She wasn't sure she even cared. Right now, all she wanted was to feel her arms around him and the wind at her back.

Sometimes the moment was all you had.

The producers were getting suspicious. That night, filming at a café in Cleveland, Jordana had guessed that one of the customers was a prostitute because of the way she was dressed. Unfortunately for Jordana, the woman turned out to be an editor at *Vogue*. The producers were not amused.

Jordana is ruining my life, Courtney lamented. She had to figure out how to get rid of her without getting both of them fired. "Can you get me some coffee?" she asked her. *Caffeine helps me think.*

"Get it yourself," Jordana barked. "Do I look like your assistant?"

Seriously, what is she good for? Courtney thought, rubbing her temples. *The least she can do is make herself useful and get me some coffee. Jordana, get me some coffee!* she mentally ordered, even though she knew that Jordana couldn't hear.

Looking a tad confused, Jordana turned to her and asked, "With or without sugar?"

"With." Courtney wasn't sure what had just happened. But she liked it.

The party at Teddy's was in full swing. He'd invited half the senior class, as well as some friends from Millennium High. It was a good thing his family had a massive loft, because there were about a hundred people there.

Cooper was talking to some groupies from Millennium when the craziest thing happened. On his right, a girl was smiling, playing with her phone. On his left, another girl was thinking, *He's cute.* But that wasn't the crazy part. Because of his ESP, he often heard girls thinking about him. The craziness started when Girl #1 thought back, *Yeah, I know. Maybe Olivia won't show up tonight. Maybe one of us can go home with him.*

Girl #2: *He has a girlfriend!*

Girl #1: *So? I'd still go home with him.*

Girl #2: *That's nasty.*

Girl #1: *Do you think he has a big nose?*

Girl #2: *It's not a great nose. But the ESP makes up for it.*

Girl #1: *I forgot about that. Can't he hear what we're thinking?*

Girl #2: Oops.

Girl# 1 (after a short pause): *Wait. I'm not talking out loud. How did you know what I was thinking?*

Girl #2 (after another short pause): *I'm not talking out loud either.*

They both looked at Cooper and started screaming.

Cooper, who had pre-gamed with a bong at home, thought he was hallucinating. How could they hear each other's thoughts? He decided he needed to lie down, and went to Teddy's room to wait for Olivia.

Teddy was in the living room, lusting after Rayna Romero, who sat next to him in homeroom. Unfortunately, she was there with Dave.

Rayna, Dave, Daniel, and Lindsay Clarke were talking in a circle in front of the fake fireplace. Lindsay was Rayna's best friend, also from 12A. They were discussing the upcoming graduation boat party.

It was an annual tradition. The Bloomberg seniors took a day-long cruise around Manhattan.

"I hope I don't get seasick," Lindsay said, clutching her stomach. "I'm not great on boats."

"I wish I had my own boat," Teddy said, edging his way into the circle.

Dave was not happy. He'd been wooing Rayna for months. Ever since she gave up her ESP back in sophomore year, she'd avoided all of us. She wanted to have a normal life. She wanted normal friends.

She also became obsessed with Taekwondo.

In order to win her over, Dave started going to her meets. It worked. He had finally convinced her to come to the party with him tonight.

And here Teddy was, trying to home in.

I really want to hook up with her, Dave heard Teddy think. *She has great boobs.*

Dave shot him a look.

Rayna glared at Teddy. "I can't believe you said that!" she spat, and punched him in the face.

It hurt. She was a green belt.

What the hell? Teddy thought. *I'm sure I didn't say that out loud.* Looking confused and more than a little stunned, he rubbed his cheek and meandered off to get some ice.

Dave was baffled. So was Daniel. How had Rayna heard that?

Lindsay, apparently, had also heard Teddy's thought. "She has great boobs?" she said. "What about me?"

Edward, in black jeans, black shoes and a black sweater, was in the kitchen getting a beer when suddenly he heard, *I shouldn't be here.* He turned around and there was Teddy, opening the freezer door. Except it wasn't Teddy's voice he'd heard in his head. It had sounded just like Isaac.

"You okay?" Edward asked, feeling disoriented.

"I, um, ran into a door," Teddy mumbled, and walked out of the kitchen, ice pack in hand.

Edward was about to leave when he heard that voice again.

This time it was loud and clear: *I'm a shit. Why am I out partying while my boyfriend is home sick in bed?*

It was definitely Isaac's voice, not Teddy's. But how could it be Isaac? Isaac was in the living room, which was on the other side of the wall.

Back in the living room, Isaac was feeling guilty about being at the party when suddenly he heard his boyfriend's voice in his head: *I can't believe Isaac believes I'm home sick. But what I am going to do now? I'm gonna have to start wearing sunglasses. Or stop screwing Kyle.*

At first, Olivia didn't think she would make it to the party. Coming back from an out-of-state basketball game, a bus carrying a load of drunk college kids had crashed on the West Side Highway, turning the ER into a warzone. No one could understand a word they were saying, so she had to stay late to make sense of their thoughts. She'd called Cooper to let him know she'd be late. It was already after nine, and she still had to go home and shower.

She was tired and didn't really want to go, but she was worried about him. He'd be smoking and drinking nonstop. She was thinking about all this when suddenly she heard him think, *What's wrong with my nose?*

She stopped in her tracks. She was ten blocks from Teddy's apartment. How could she possibly have heard that?

She strained to hear more, but the transmission had stopped. She began to panic. *Why* had it stopped? Had something happened to him? What if he had a stroke? Teens had strokes too, she knew. Lots of them. She'd read somewhere that stroke rates had gone up by 30 per cent for kids. And Cooper smoked a lot. That was one of the risk factors, wasn't it? She was pretty sure it was.

To her relief, when she arrived at the party, she found him snoring in Teddy's bed. Chalking up what she'd heard to exhaustion, she took off her shoes and climbed in next to him.

Michelle was sitting on a couch in the living room, wondering why no one was paying any attention to her. *Why don't guys like me? Where is my Prince Charming? Am I ever going to meet him? Does he even exist?*

Lately, with prom coming up, she'd been thinking a lot about royalty. Specifically why, unlike most high schools in the country, New York schools didn't have prom queens. How unfair was that?

She thought she'd make a great queen. She even had the wave down.

But anyway. Her prince was never coming. She glanced at the boy sitting next to her. She didn't know him – probably one of Teddy's friends from Millennium. He was kind of cute, she thought. He was a redhead. She liked redheads. Prince Harry was a redhead.

She was done waiting. She cleared her throat. "Hi," she said. "I'm Michelle."

He nodded.

"Are you friends with Teddy?"

He nodded again.

She slumped back into the couch. *I'm not good at this. I'll never hook up with anyone. I will die a virgin.* Then she got angry. Fine, he wasn't interested. She could accept that. But not to even acknowledge her presence? What made him think he was so superior? He wasn't actually a prince. He was hurting her feelings. That was just plain rude.

She tried again.

"What school do you go to? I haven't seen you around."

This time he didn't even look at her.

Look at me, you miserable jerk! she mentally commanded.

He turned to look at her.

They stared at each other. Had he heard her? Why had he done what she said? Would he do anything she said?

Say something.

"Hello," he said.

Tell me your name, she demanded.

"Joshua," he replied.

Huh, she thought. He seemed to respond to thoughts that contained commands.

A slow grin curled her lips.

Kiss me, she thought.

I think I'm going to kiss her, he thought. And then he did.

Sitting across from them on the red sofa, Levi had just struck out with Lindsay and was now hitting on Parisa Myers, who was also from 12A. But that wasn't working either, and he was feeling pretty low.

Where were all his groupies? Had the novelty worn off?

He'd overheard what happened to Michelle – who was still making out with Joshua – and had been blown away for two reasons: one, she seemed to have developed some kind of new power; and two, she was making out with a total stranger.

Just then, Clancy, Teddy's cocker spaniel, padded over and licked Levi's shoes.

And then he had an idea. He was in Michelle's group! Maybe it would work for him?

Sit, he commanded.

Clancy sat.

Roll over.

Clancy rolled over.

Holy smokes, it worked!

He turned to Parisa. *You want me. Come with me to the den immediately.*

I want him… to drop dead, she thought, and got up to leave.

It was almost 3 a.m., and the party was winding down. Some of us were wasted. Most of us were tired. All of us were confused. Especially Tess and BJ. For some reason, they were the only Espies at the party whose ESP hadn't gone haywire.

What was going on? Was it even safe?

We mentally communicated to convene in the den. Except for Cooper and Olivia, who were still asleep in Teddy's room. We began discussing the situation.

I can hear through walls, Edward thought.

So what? Isaac thought. *I can hear long distance.*

I can make people do things, Michelle thought.

I can make dogs do things, Levi thought.

People near me can hear each other, Dave and Daniel thought simultaneously.

Tess and BJ felt left out. None of this was happening to them. BJ pulled out his phone.

"What are you doing?" Levi asked.

"I'm texting the others. We need to set up a meeting. With *all* the Espies." *I need to find out why I didn't get an enhancement.*

Dave groaned. "No more morning meetings!"

BJ thought for a moment. "Is Cooper's dad away again?"

"He's always away," Levi pointed out. "He's a consultant."

"When do Courtney and Jordana get back from Cleveland?"

"Not sure. Some time tomorrow night. Maybe nine?"

BJ sent a group text:

```
Emergency meeting, 10 p.m. Sunday
at Cooper's. Mandatory.
```

"I'll text the others again tomorrow," he said. "Just to make sure everyone comes."

Courtney texted back immediately, saying she'd be coming straight from the airport. She knew what it was about. She'd been having symptoms, too. Like making-Jordana-do-things-for-her symptoms. Not that Courtney was complaining.

"Maybe we should wake up Cooper," Levi said. "He probably should know we volunteered his apartment."

"Why do we even have to meet?" Daniel whined. "Why can't we just talk about it now? We can text the others later."

"Because we need help," BJ said. "And we need answers."

We needed Pi.

Chapter Eighteen
DEATH SURGES AND DUDS

"I should sue you for sleep deprivation," Courtney was complaining. We were sitting in a circle, in the middle of Cooper's living room. It was close to midnight and we were all tired. "Tomorrow's a school day. I need my beauty sleep."

"In that case," Levi said, "you should probably sleep through summer."

Bite me, Levi.

Edward will bite you, Levi thought back.

I totally would, thought Edward.

"Why are we here again?" Jordana asked, yawning.

"Because this is an emergency," Pi said. "We might be in danger." *I have no idea why she's here. It's not like her ESP is coming back.*

"I can hear long distance," Isaac said. "What's dangerous

150

about that? You wanted to stimulate the NFG. It's stimulated. Seems the experiment is working."

Pi shook her head. "Just because you have extra powers doesn't mean you won't eventually *lose* your ESP. This could be temporary. It could be a death surge."

"What's a death surge?" Mona asked.

Olivia turned pale. "It's when terminally ill patients get a surge of energy just before they die."

"Oh. My. God," Courtney said. "Are we going to die?"

Pi rolled her eyes. "No one's dying, okay? I was talking about our ESP."

There was a lot of mental musing, and then everyone got quiet.

"Okay, listen up," Pi said. "After listening to each of your stories, I have concluded that four of the six groups have been enhanced."

Duh, Dave thought.

"Let's start with Group 1," Pi said, ignoring him. "All those who can hear through walls, please raise your hands."

Mackenzie, Edward, and Brinn shot up their arms.

"Brinn heard me through the bathroom wall," Mackenzie said. "Are you saying it's because of the magnesium?"

"You were ES*Pee*ing," Cooper joked, and we all groaned.

"I think—" Brinn started.

"Exactly," Pi said to Mackenzie, cutting Brinn off. She turned to the others. "I want everyone to take note. The entire group has been enhanced. Therefore, it was the magnesium that caused it. Magnesium makes Espies hear through walls."

"But remember when we first got ESP?" Jordana asked. "I could hear through walls a little, too. I wasn't taking magnesium."

"Maybe you were just eating something with a lot of magnesium in it," Pi said.

"Like what?"

"Pumpkin seeds? Almonds?"

"Oh! I *was* drinking almond milk for a while. A lot of it. Could that have done it?"

"Yes," Pi said. "Why'd you stop?"

"I didn't like the taste," she said. But she thought, *It gave me cold sores.*

Ew. Does Jordana have herpes?

Cold sores aren't herpes!

Yes, they are, Olivia thought. *The HSV-1 strain.*

I don't want any kind of strain.

"Wait," said Mackenzie. "I've been taking magnesium all my life. Are you saying it was the magnesium that made me hear through walls to begin with?" *I'm not special?*

Yes, Pi thought. *That's exactly what I'm saying. If I'd been the one taking magnesium, then I'd have been number one in Lab all along.*

"So that's why my ESP got stronger?" Mackenzie asked. "Because I'm taking more?"

"Yes. Didn't you say you heard your boyfriend through the convenience store wall? You were about fifty feet away, right?"

Your boyfriend? Cooper thought. *Now he's your boyfriend?*

Olivia gave Cooper a look. *What does he care? Why is he still obsessing over Mackenzie?* It was enough. So she had a new boyfriend. He had Olivia.

"He's not my boyfriend!" Mackenzie said.

"I'm not obsessing!" Cooper said.

Olivia picked at her thumbnail.

"Okay, moving on," Pi said. She glanced down at her iPad. "Group 2. Gingko. Cooper, Daniel and Dave. Telepathic relay, right?"

We had no idea what she was talking about. Telepathic relay?

"You mean like a race?" Dave asked.

"No, Dave," Pi said. "Pay attention. I'm not talking about a relay race, obviously. Telepathic relay is when you act as a mental hub for other people. They get to communicate with each other through you."

We just stared.

Pi sighed. *Why are they so dense?* "Dave, didn't you say that Rayna got upset when she heard Teddy thinking about her breasts?"

I believe he used the word "boobs".

He's classy that way.

That was a good punch. Maybe I should take Taekwondo.

"Then there were those groupies from Millennium," Pi said, turning to Cooper. "They heard each other, too."

"I still don't get it," Cooper said. "What's wrong with my nose?"

It's not the smallest.

It leans to the right.

It's attached to your face.

"Look, here's how it works," Pi said, scribbling on her iPad. A few seconds later, our phones buzzed and an illustration popped up in our emails:

"What are you, five?" Sadie asked.

"I said I'd explain," Pi snapped. "I never said I was Rembrandt."

"Why did you make me so short?" Daniel asked. "I should be the same height as Dave."

"And why does Lindsay have pigtails?" Courtney asked. "Lindsay doesn't wear pigtails. Ever."

Pi blew out a breath. "Guys, you're missing the point. I'm trying to show you how Rayna and Lindsay heard what Teddy was thinking. Look where they're standing. Dave is between Rayna and Teddy, and Daniel is between Teddy and Lindsay. Rayna heard Teddy through Dave, and Lindsay heard Teddy through Daniel."

"That hurts my head," Cooper said.

It's called a hangover, Sadie thought.

"Next is Group 3," Pi said. "Lutein. Long distance. People?"

Olivia, Isaac, and Mona all shouted, "Me!"

"So how's it different from hearing through walls?" Mackenzie asked.

"It's a lot more powerful," Pi said. "You can hear through walls *and* be far away."

"Can I hear people in China?" Mona asked.

What about the girls' locker room?

Who does she know in China?

"China is probably too far," Pi said. "Isaac, can you do a distance test for us?"

"I don't know anyone in China," he said.

"Isaac. Think. Pick somewhere else. It just has to be somewhere far away."

His face brightened. "I have a cousin in Vegas. Is Vegas okay?"

"Yes, Isaac. Vegas is fine."

We all waited.

"And?" Pi asked.

"I can't hear him," Isaac said.

"You have to be totally focused," Olivia said. "When I heard Cooper's thoughts, I was thinking about him really hard."

Cooper smiled at her. *That's sweet.*

She smiled back.

She's right, Isaac thought. *When I first heard Richard, I was thinking about him and feeling bad that he was home sick.* He scrunched up his face and tried again. "Still nothing. My cousin is probably asleep. His eyes still have to be open, right?"

"It's only nine thirty in the evening in Vegas," Pi said. "Why would he be asleep?" She thought for a moment. "Call him. And think about him hard. That way we'll know for sure."

Isaac picked up his cell and punched in a number. "Hello, Max? It's me... Your cousin Isaac?... Yes, Isaac from New York... No, Grandma is still alive... What do you mean, why am I calling? To say hi... Oh. Okay. Sorry."

"And?" Pi asked.

"He was asleep. I woke him up."

Who goes to sleep at nine thirty in Vegas?

"Isaac, what was he thinking?"

"Oh. Right. I don't know. I couldn't hear."

"Well, that answers that," Pi said. "The range is limited."

"It's still better than hearing through walls," Mona said, gloating. "Go Team Lutein!"

Mars made a sad face.

"Okay, last one," Pi said. "Group 6. Cognizin citicoline. This one is really spectacular. Michelle, do you want to talk, or should I?"

Michelle turned red.

"Fine, then," Pi said, when Michelle didn't answer. "With this enhancement, you get to plant your thoughts in someone's head and make them think they're their own. But it seems to only work if you include some kind of command. In other words, you *push* the thoughts into the other person's mind. And that's where it gets interesting," she added, smirking at Michelle. "You think, 'Kiss me!' and he thinks, 'Maybe I should kiss her.' You can basically get them to do what you want."

"Like bring you coffee," Courtney said. *Even though Jordana forgot the sugar.*

"I don't understand," Levi said. "I'm in that group, too. I tried it on Parisa, and nothing happened. But it worked on Teddy's dog."

I think you and Teddy's dog would make a great couple.

"Oh, Parisa got the message," Pi said. "But it's kind of like hypnosis. You can't get someone to do something they don't really want to do." She gave him a stern look. "So quit being an asshole, okay? Do not, I repeat, DO NOT use this power to get anyone to make out with you. That goes for you too, Michelle."

Michelle turned redder.

"What about me?" BJ asked. "How come I'm not enhanced?"

That's not what Tess thinks.

Shut up, you perv.

Pi frowned. "Don't feel bad, neither am I. It looks like Groups 4 and 5 are duds." *I can't believe I ended up with the losers.*

"I want to switch groups," Jordana announced. "I want to be enhanced!"

"You don't even have ESP," Pi said. "There's nothing to enhance. Just focus on getting it back." *It'll never happen.*

"I want to be in Pi's group," Olivia said. "What if the lutein is giving me a death surge? I don't care about the enhancements. I just don't want to lose my ESP." *I don't want to lose my ESP. I don't want to lose my ESP. Pick. Pick. Pick.*

"I didn't say it *was* a death surge," Pi said. "I said it *could* be a death surge." *And can you stop picking your fingers? It's disgusting.*

More disgusting than Jordana's cold sores?

Guys, don't make fun of Jordana! It's not fair! She can't hear!

"Mona wants to change groups, too," Mars said. "Right, Mona?" *We don't care about the enhancements, either. We just want to be together.*

What? No. I want to hear long distance! "It's okay," Mona said. "I can stay where I am."

Don't you want to be with me?

I do! You switch.

"I don't want to move, either," Michelle said, then blushed again.

Of course Pi wanted to have an enhancement, but that wasn't the goal of this experiment. The goal was to keep her ESP. "We need to stick to my original plan," she said, somewhat dejectedly. "We are taking very high dosages of the supplements and having serious reactions. We shouldn't make any adjustments until we know exactly what we're dealing with. Once we figure out how to keep our telepathy from going away, we can think about switching or taking one or two extra supplements. But for now, we need to keep our priorities straight. We need to focus on saving our ESP. You can't have enhanced ESP if there's nothing to enhance."

Fine.

Whatever.

"So we're clear?" Pi said. "No one's switching groups, and no one's taking additional supplements."

"That goes for you, too," Levi said to Pi, giving her a threatening look.

"Oh, I'm so scared," she said. "Not."

Maybe Levi should take Taekwondo.

Except Pi *was* scared. Not of Levi, obviously, but of this latest turn of events. What didn't kill you made you stronger, but it could kill you just the same.

Chapter Nineteen
POKER FACE

It was a week of enhancements.

On Tuesday, Brinn was all dressed up in her fencing gear and was about to enter the gym when she heard Donald Witherspoon thinking through the door: *I hope Brinn doesn't show up today. Last week she nearly decapitated me. That girl has anger issues. Someone should kick her out of the club.*

Brinn got angry.

She not so accidentally decapitated his backpack.

Isaac spent the week obsessing over Richard, listening to him long distance twenty-four-seven. Actually, it was more like sixteen-seven, since you couldn't hear people when they were asleep. What kind of person cheated on you a month before prom?

A jerk! Stop thinking about him!

Mona spent the week annoyed with Mars. He was still upset that she'd chosen hearing long distance over being with him. Not that she'd really had a choice. But did he consider that? No, he did not. She was starting to think he was a bit of a control freak.

He totally is.

I am not!

And Michelle… Well, Michelle was over wannabe Prince Harry. Instead, she had decided to take matters into her own hands. She didn't want to find her prince. She wanted to be a princess.

A prom princess.

She wanted to be prom queen.

The issue was that Bloomberg High didn't have a prom queen or king. So she went to see Principal Roth.

"I have an idea," she said. "Bloomberg High should have a prom queen and king."

That seems like a lot of work, Principal Roth thought. *And I need to post that picture of my breakfast on Instagram.*

Listen to me, lazy old man, Michelle commanded. *We're gonna have a prom king and queen. Make it happen. And I better be one of the nominations. Got it?*

"A prom queen and king," he said, nodding. "I'm going to make it happen. And you will be one of the nominations."

The truth was, he had always had a soft spot for royalty. His first crush had been Princess Diana.

On Saturday morning, Mackenzie's brother and sister came

home to visit. Their mother was having surgery on Monday, and they wanted to be with her when she woke up. Perfectly understandable, but what Mackenzie didn't get was why they had to be so annoying. *Why does Mackenzie's shirt have holes in it? She's a mess as usual. It's because Mom isn't here to do her laundry. She should really learn to do her own laundry. Why do they baby her so much? She'll last two weeks at Stanford, tops...* Because her powers were enhanced, she could even hear them across the hallway, through their respective bedroom walls: *I can't believe she's going out tonight. How often does she get to see us? How can she even consider going out two days before the operation? Mom and Dad let her get away with murder.*

Mackenzie put on sunglasses, marched outside and parked herself right on the back of Bennett's motorcycle. *Ahhhh. Wind. Noise.*

So what if she ended up at his Brooklyn apartment afterwards? She put the music on loud and kept her eyes closed.

Courtney decided to put her enhancement to work. They were filming in a jewelry store in Los Angeles when a man came in to buy his girlfriend a necklace. Problem was, he was already married. *Jerkface has a wife*, Courtney thought, staring straight at Jordana. But Jordana just stared back, looking a little dazed. Why wasn't it working? Then Courtney remembered that she had to include a command. *Tell Jerkface to give the necklace to his wife*, she thought at Jordana. "Give the necklace to your wife," Jordana said, still in a daze.

He looked like he was going to be sick.

And then Courtney had an idea. What if she could save his marriage? *You need to send a text*, she thought in his direction. *Tell your girlfriend it's over.*

Not only did he look sick, he seemed confused. "Which girlfriend?" he asked. "Allison or Amanda?"

Olivia knew listening to Cooper's thoughts was kind of like reading his diary.

She tried to stop.

She really did.

But she couldn't help it. She thought about him while she was walking down the street. She thought about him while she was eating breakfast. She thought about him while she cleaned her room. She thought about him and POOF! there he was in her head.

On Saturday afternoon, while she washed her lunch dishes, she listened in on him on his train to Jersey. He was thinking about his next poker game.

He loved those poker games. She wished he would stop. She also wished he would stop smoking pot.

But she still loved him.

After drying her fork, she went to sit down at her computer.

She looked at the letter she'd gotten the day before.

Johns Hopkins was giving her a full scholarship. They had a pre-med program. NYU didn't.

Her dream school was giving her a full scholarship!

Part of her was thrilled. The other part of her was miserable.

Now what was she supposed to do?

She could stay in New York. She could be with Cooper. NYU was a great school. She'd get to live at home.

But she didn't want to live at home. She wanted to live in a dorm and go to her dream school.

But then she'd have to leave Cooper. She didn't want to leave Cooper.

Olivia was worried that if she didn't stay with him, they wouldn't make it as a couple. Everyone knew long distance was a killer. What if he forgot about her? What if he met some tall, blond girl with long legs and no mental issues?

She picked her thumb.

No. If she wanted to keep him, she had to be with him. She had to go NYU. She had to stay in New York.

She sighed and looked out the window.

Of course, she could still lose him. What if she stayed in New York, and then he dumped her, anyway? What if he dumped her and decided to get back together with Mackenzie? What if one of his poker buddies uncovered who he was and threw him off a bridge?

He'd be dead. She'd be alone and stuck in New York. What if she lost her ESP? Getting into med school would be tougher. What if she never got to be a doctor?

Pick. Pick. Pick.

If she went away to school he would forget about her for sure. They'd be done. She knew it deep in her bones.

Sure, he liked her. She knew he liked her. He thought about her when she wasn't there. Just yesterday, he'd been thinking about her. She knew he'd been thinking about her because she'd been listening to him.

But he thought things like, *I wonder what Olivia's doing*. Or, *Maybe Olivia wants to come over*. Not: *I need to see Olivia right this second or I'm going to die*.

He wasn't obsessed with her. Not the way she was with him.

She didn't know what to do. What should she do?

"How's your father?" Cooper's mom asked later that day in New Jersey. "Still working too much?" *Still whoring around?* She'd remarried, but still hated her ex with a raging passion.

Cooper shrugged. Earlier that morning, his dad had come home to find the apartment in shambles. Ten straight days of partying will do that, but what we couldn't figure out was why Cooper didn't even bother to clean up. Not that his father seemed to care. Barely an hour after he'd arrived home, he said he was off again and wouldn't be back until Tuesday. *Bethany's going to be pissed*, he thought, as he rushed out the door. *She was expecting me an hour ago.*

"Yeah," Cooper said. "Same old Dad."

"You two getting along?" his mom asked. "Or is he being a jerk to you, too?"

"It's all good," Cooper answered, forcing a smile.

She nodded. "I'm glad. And how's Olivia?"

"She's good, too," he said.

He wasn't sure if that was true.

She'd started to pick her fingers a lot.

She was worried about the future.

Cooper didn't want to think about the future. He didn't want to think at all. He wanted to play poker. Winning was so easy.

Everything was so easy.

He'd gotten into NYU and his dad was paying. He had a great girlfriend who loved him. Did he deserve it?

We didn't think so. He wasn't so sure either.

Sometimes he wondered if he wanted to get caught. If he wanted the guys to beat the crap out of him. If he wanted his mother to realize how much pot he was smoking. If he wanted his father to come home during a party and get pissed off. If he wanted Olivia to yell at him for being a terrible boyfriend.

Sometimes he wondered if he even wanted to get out of bed.

That night at poker he won the first hand. Of course he did. He lost the second on purpose then won the third.

It was easy. So easy. Everything was easy. What was the point?

What was the point of anything?

He picked up a chicken wing. The chicken wings were good. Were they the point?

"You gonna draw or what?" Alan, the guy on his right, was asking. "Earth to Leo. You in or out?"

"Yeah, sorry," Cooper said, and picked up two cards.

I think Alan is cheating, thought Jarred, the guy on his left.

"Did you just call me a cheater?" Alan asked Jarred.

Did I say that out loud? I'm sure I didn't say it out loud. "Screw you, man."

Asshole, Alan thought.

"What did you call me?" Jarred said.

Realizing what was happening, Cooper put down his cards. *Shit.* Alan and Jarred could hear each other's thoughts. It was that damn relay thing, and Cooper was the hub. Alan was sitting on his left, Jarred on his right. "I fold," he said, and pushed away from table.

He knew right away that his poker days were over. What choice did he have? It wasn't like he could wear sunglasses at the table. Players kind of balked at tactics like that. Poker was a game of bluffing, and the eyes spoke volumes.

Besides, if he wore sunglasses, he wouldn't be able to win.

"Christ, what *was* that?" Jarred asked Alan. "It was like I could read your mind."

"You and me both," Alan said.

"We must have been talking, right?" Jarred looked at the others. "Did you guys see my lips move?"

"I thought I saw them twitch," said one of the others. "They always twitch when you're bluffing."

"Maybe you have that ESP thing like those freaks in the city," one of the other guys said.

"You better not," said a third. "Not unless you want me to kick your teeth in."

They all started laughing.

"Too much beer, man," Jarred said, shaking his head.

"I guess," Alan said. "And maybe we should lay off the ganja."

Cooper's heart raced. He didn't *really* want to get the shit kicked out of him. *I have to get out of here*, he thought. "I think I ate too many chicken wings," he said. "My stomach's not great."

Then he took off.

Olivia heaved a sigh of relief.

And then there were the duds.

Sadie didn't care that she wasn't enhanced. She already had everything she wanted – she was going to Columbia in the fall, and Dumbo was crazy about her. She didn't even care that she had ESP, to be honest.

Although she was smart enough not to say that last part out loud.

As for Tess and BJ, nothing much had changed. They spent Saturday on Pier 25, which jutted out into the Hudson. They found chairs that faced the water, lay down and soaked up the breeze and sunshine.

I love you.

I love you, too.

Let's go home and have sex.

BJ!

Like Sadie, they didn't care that they weren't enhanced. They were just glad they had each other. Sure, we all had ESP, but they had each other *and* ESP. You couldn't get much closer than that.

Tess was grateful they both still had their telepathy. She was also grateful they were in the same group. This way, whatever happened would happen to both of them.

Or not.

Chapter Twenty
THE AGE OF INNOCENCE

It was 5:20 p.m. on Monday, and Mackenzie's mother was still in surgery. Her doctor was confident that her voice box could be saved, and even though he'd assured them that the procedure was less extensive than a full laryngectomy, they were all nervous. Surgery was still surgery.

If it wasn't as extensive, then what was taking so long?

Mackenzie had forgotten her sunglasses. At first it didn't matter. She wanted to get a heads-up on what the doctors were thinking, anyway. But then she realized that there in the waiting room, she was too far away to hear what was going on. And, unfortunately, she could still hear the thoughts of everyone around her. *The gallstone was the size of a basketball... I wonder if the doctors here hook up with each other as much as they do on* Grey's Anatomy... *That needle they gave him was the size of a tree trunk...*

One more mention of needles, and she'd be passed out on the waiting room floor.

Mackenzie leaned back in her chair and closed her eyes.

When she woke up, it was an hour later and the waiting room was empty. In a panic, she ran up and down the hallway, looking for her family.

"Where were you?" she demanded, when she saw them approach. "Did something happen? Is there any news?"

"We went to the coffee shop," her brother said. "We brought you back a sandwich."

"Do you want to go home, sweetie?" her dad asked. *She must be tired.*

Poor little Mackenzie, her sister thought. *Yeah. I know you can hear me.*

"We're all tired, Dad," Mackenzie said, ignoring her sister. She was probably just being extra bitchy because she was worried about their mother. "Is there any news?"

Her father shook his head. "No news." His face was pinched, his brow furrowed.

Mackenzie's heart went out to him. He looked so worried. Why wasn't anyone coming by with an update? What was going on?

She had half a mind to go down to the OR and listen through the walls; the other half, the half that recoiled at the sight of blood, screamed, "No!"

They went back to the waiting room. Her siblings and father sat in a row by the window while Mackenzie sat across from them, as far away as possible.

She needed a distraction.

Homework. She would do some homework.

She pulled out the book she was supposed to read for English. *The Age of Innocence*. Chapter One. On a January evening in the early seventies...

I bet she doesn't eat unless Mom and Dad feed her, her sister thought, nibbling on a donut.

Apparently, she wasn't far enough.

The next few hours passed. To Mackenzie's surprise, she found she was really into the story. She was engrossed in a scene when she heard someone come into the waiting room. Thinking it might be a doctor, she looked up to see Cooper. He said hello to her family, talked with them for a minute, and then came over to Mackenzie.

"Hey," she said, looking up at him. "What are you doing here?"

He gave her a lopsided smile. "Isn't this the hot new hang-out spot in the city? Thought I read something about it in *Time Out*," he said, and sat down next to her.

She raised an eyebrow.

"I thought you could use a little distraction."

She grimaced. *Well, you got that right. My family is driving me crazy.*

I wouldn't worry about it, Cooper thought. *Sanity is highly overrated. Have you heard anything?*

She shook her head. *No, nothing. No one's been out to talk to us.*

He glanced at the book on her lap. "How's the book?" he asked.

"Pretty good," she said. "Have you read it yet?"

"No. Isn't there a movie?"

"I think so. But you should try it. It's good."

He laughed. "I've never seen you read a book before."

"I know! Thought I'd read at least one before I graduate."

"How does it end?"

"I don't know yet. Right now, the main guy – Archer – goes down to the shore to look for Ellen, the woman he's in love with. He sees her standing on the pier and wonders if she knows he's watching her. Then he sees a sailboat and decides that if she doesn't turn around before it passes the lighthouse, he'll leave without saying a word."

Cooper fake-yawned. "Any more intense, I'd have a heart attack."

"Good thing the ER is downstairs."

"So what happens next?" he asked. "Does she turn around or not?"

Mackenzie sighed. "No, he waits and waits, but she doesn't even move, so he leaves."

"Sad," he said.

"Yeah. Sad. But romantic." Her voice got quiet. A memory trickled into her mind. It was a Saturday afternoon, and she was sitting on a bench, waiting for Cooper in Battery Park. When he finally showed up, he was carrying a bouquet of wildflowers and whistling a cheesy show tune. He was half an hour late, but he had a good excuse. It wasn't easy finding wildflowers in Manhattan. She'd never loved him more.

You were wearing a yellow dress. You'd just cut your hair and were afraid I wouldn't like it.

Did you like it?

Their eyes locked. *Of course. You looked beautiful. You always did. You always do.*

They sat in silence. He cleared his throat. "I should get going."

"Where are you off to?"

"Olivia is working in the children's ward. I'm meeting her in the lobby."

Oh. That's why he's here. I thought he came to see me.

I did come to see you.

You know what I mean.

"Mackenzie…" he started, but then stopped. What was there to say? He tapped the armrests with his fingers.

"Sorry," she said, shaking her head. "I appreciate you coming. It was good to see a friendly face." She felt a surge of emotion. *I miss you.*

I miss you, too, he thought.

Another surge. *You do?*

He flushed. *Of course I do. You were my best friend.*

You were mine, she thought. *Do you remember when we met?*

He snapped his fingers. *Nursery. You were crying because you missed your mom.*

You gave me a cookie to cheer me up!

You told me oatmeal cookies weren't real cookies and to come back when I had a chocolate chip one.

Mackenzie laughed. *I was such a bitch! I can't believe you were so nice to me.*

No, you were right. I hated oatmeal cookies, too. He smiled as another memory came to him. *Remember when I snuck out of my fire escape to watch the eclipse with you?*

She smiled. *What were we, ten?*

Twelve. I can't believe I got away with that.

What about the time my parents caught us making out? You ran out of my room so fast you were like the Road Runner. Practically made a hole in the wall.

He looked down at the floor. She'd shifted the conversation back to when they were dating, and he didn't know how to respond.

You broke my heart, he thought.

Her eyes filled with tears. *I'm sorry.*

He nodded. *I know. We were young. You were scared.*

I'm still scared. Her throat tightened and she felt sick. *My mom, Cooper, my mom!*

He reached over and smoothed the hair around her face. It was a simple gesture, but it made tears spill down her cheeks.

He put his arms around her and let her cry on his shoulder.

When a doctor in scrubs came into the waiting room. Cooper pulled back and took Mackenzie's hand. They walked over to the window where her family was seated.

Mackenzie held her breath.

"She did great," the doctor said. "We did have to remove part of her larynx, but we're hoping she'll regain her speech soon."

"Hoping?" Cailin asked.

"Yes," the doctor said. "She won't sound quite the same, but we're extremely optimistic about the results. She can start speech therapy as soon we remove the tracheostomy tube."

"What about the cancer?" her father asked. That was the real question. The one they were all afraid to ask.

"We believe we got it all."

Mackenzie's father sank into his chair. His shoulders sagged with relief.

"Can we see her?" Cailin asked.

"Not right away. She's still in recovery. We'll let you know when she wakes up."

Cooper squeezed Mackenzie's hand. Mackenzie squeezed back.

Mackenzie was all choked up. Her mother was going to be okay.

"You should go home now," her dad said to her. "You're probably exhausted. We'll call you when she wakes up."

There he goes, babying her again, Cailin thought. *Although she does look kind of tired*. "Yeah, Mackenzie. We've got it covered," she said.

"I'm staying right here," Mackenzie said, suppressing a smile. They were annoying, but they were still family. At least they were always there for her.

Cooper squeezed her hand again. *I'm always here for you, too.*

Olivia was in the children's ward when she heard Cooper's thoughts. She'd been reading to five-year-old Fiona from the fourth book in the *Ivy & Bean* series.

Cooper missed Mackenzie? He would always be there for her? What was wrong with oatmeal cookies? Olivia loved oatmeal cookies.

She'd also picked up a few of Mackenzie's thoughts, and was now feeling sick to her stomach. It was obvious Mackenzie wanted him back.

Olivia knew Cooper would be stopping by the waiting room. It wasn't like he'd tried to hide it. She also knew that she should probably go down there, too. It was the right thing to do. But she couldn't. She couldn't face them.

Mackenzie had a power over him that Olivia had never understood, and how could you compete with something you didn't understand?

Wasn't their little tête-à-tête in the waiting room proof enough?

What would happen now? Would he realize he was still in love with Mackenzie? Would he keep denying it – to her and to himself – and string Olivia along? For how long? The rest of the school year? Over the summer? What about next year? Should she just go to Johns Hopkins and call it a day? What if she lost her ESP? What if she lost everything? What should she do? Go to Johns Hopkins? Go to NYU? She had to make a decision before they gave her scholarships away.

She felt cold. And lightheaded.

Was she going to pass out? She was going to pass out.

"Keep reading!" Fiona demanded, motioning to the book in Olivia's lap. "Why did you stop?" *Olivia looks funny,* she thought. *Maybe she has a hernia, too.*

Do not pass out. Do not pass out. You are here to learn to be a doctor, not become a patient. Get it together.

"I'm sorry," Olivia said, her hands shaking.

"Were you daydreaming about your boyfriend?"

"Yes," she said. But it wasn't a daydream. It was a nightmare.

Chapter Twenty-One
LIAR, LIAR, PANTS ON FIRE

That night, Tess's mother was going to a show with a few colleagues from work and wouldn't be home for hours. She reminded Tess that BJ wasn't allowed over while she was out. Also, that Tess was not to sample the cookies on the kitchen table. They were for her book club tomorrow. "You might want to think about watching the snacks before prom," she said on the way out. "You'll have those pictures forever, you know."

Tess had her mother's dark olive skin, but much to her mother's disappointment, not her tiny dress size. Tess no longer cared what her mother thought. She was quite happy with her body. Plus, BJ believed she was the sexiest woman alive.

Tess ignored her mother entirely. She popped a cookie in her mouth as soon as her mom was out the door and then invited BJ over.

A text popped up from Olivia.

```
Do you have time to talk?
```

She typed back while munching.

```
BJ on his way over. Can it wait
until tomorrow? Everything okay?
```

Three dots.
Tess waited. She ate another cookie.

```
Olivia: Yeah. Can you meet me
before homeroom in the cafeteria?
Tess: Okay.
```

Later, while BJ played with her hair, Tess wondered why Olivia wanted to meet. They were friends, but not best friends. These days Olivia spent most of her time with Cooper.

"What time did you say your mom will be home?" BJ asked, nibbling on her ear.

"What if Olivia lost her ESP?"

"It's not her ESP," BJ said, moving down to her neck. "She would have texted everyone."

"Probably," Tess said, turning to look at him. "Maybe it has something to do with Cooper. Did you see him at Teddy's party? He was beyond wasted."

"I'm still hungover myself," BJ said. "I might need medical

attention, doctor. Maybe a little mouth-to-mouth?"

"That must be some hangover. The party was a week ago."
Then she frowned. "Are you really not feeling well?" She put
her hand to his forehead. "You're not getting sick, are you?
You can't get sick – the party boat is in a few weeks, and then
there's prom, and then—"

"I do feel a little dizzy," he interrupted. "I might roll onto
the floor. Maybe you should tie me to the bed and—"

She sat up and hit him with her pillow. "Can you be serious
for a minute? Are you okay or not?"

"Ooh, the lady likes it rough," he said, tossing the pillow
back at her. "I'm fine," he said. *At least I will be as soon as we
get naked.*

"But what about Olivia?"

"She can get naked, too, if she wants."

She laughed. "You wish." She rolled over and planted
a big, juicy kiss on his lips. He was a pervert, but he was
her pervert.

After BJ left Tess's, he went to McDonald's.

It happened while he was waiting in line. He was getting a
Chicken McWrap. He loved the McWraps. He had at least one
a day, sometimes for breakfast, sometimes as a late-night snack.

But not tonight. Tonight, he ran straight back to Tess's
apartment.

Tess was sitting on her couch having some tea and writing
in her diary. She loved to drink tea while she wrote. It felt like
such a writerly thing to do.

Her mom had just come home and was about to get ready for bed. "How many cookies did you have?" she asked, glancing at the plate on the coffee table.

"Just a few," Tess droned. She didn't add that BJ had had a few, too.

Before her mother could reply, Tess's phone rang.

"It's me," BJ said. "I'm in the lobby. We need to talk."

"Come up," she said. "But I have to warn you, she's home."

Her mother raised an eyebrow.

"No," he said. "You come down. It's private."

"Okay, just give me a sec," she said, suddenly anxious. What was so important – and private – that couldn't wait until morning?

"Was that BJ?" her mother asked, brightening. She liked BJ. A lot. Of course, it didn't hurt that he flirted with her.

"Yeah," Tess said, throwing on a sweater. "We're going for a walk."

"But it's almost eleven!" Though really, her mother looked more disappointed than worried. "Why can't he come up?"

"I don't know! He wants me to come down."

"Well, I hope you're going to change. At least put on some lipstick."

Tess resisted the urge to laugh. She didn't think he'd care that she was wearing sweatpants. Not after seeing her naked.

As soon as she stepped out of the elevator, she knew something was wrong. It was written all over his face. His eyebrows were pushed together, his forehead deeply etched.

Shit, he thought.

What happened?

He kept clenching and unclenching his fists.

BJ?

He didn't answer.

She felt cold all over. *Say something, damn it!*

Shit, shit, shit.

"What happened?" she asked again, this time out loud.

She knew what he would say, even without his thinking it.

"It's gone."

"When?" she asked.

"I was getting a McWrap."

"After you left here, you went to McDonald's?"

He shrugged. "I was hungry."

"And?" She waited for him to continue.

"I was listening to the girl in front of me have this debate with herself about whether the guy she'd hooked up with was going to call. Should she have slept with him on the first date? Should she call him? Should she text him? Should she show up at his apartment? And then suddenly I got this intense pain in my head and I started to get dizzy—"

"Omigod," Tess said. "You were feeling dizzy earlier tonight. I thought you were joking!"

His lips twitched. "I was a little dizzy, but then it passed. And then it came back."

"It did?"

"At first. But then I couldn't hear anything at all. And the worst part? The girl's phone rang a second later and I didn't know if it was him!"

"That's the worst part?" Tess asked.

No! I mean, yes. I mean, I'm so used to knowing stuff automatically and now I can't know anything at all. I can't believe this happened. What do I do now?

"We'll figure it out together," Tess said with more confidence than she felt. What was to figure out? His ESP was gone. Dead. Defunct. "Everything's going to be all right." Would it? That part of their life, that special bond, was over. How could it be all right?

He jumped back. "You can still hear me?"

"Of course I can still hear you." What did he think? He knew how this worked. She hadn't lost her powers. She could still hear everyone.

I don't want her listening to me if I can't listen to her.

"I'm sorry," she said, feeling a little put off. "There's nothing I can do about it."

"Stop it!" BJ said. *I don't want her to hear me!*

"You're acting crazy," Tess snapped. But then she felt bad. He was upset. He was lashing out. Who knew how she'd react if the situation were reversed?

I need to get out of here.

"I'll come with you. We'll talk more."

He shook his head. "No. I need to be alone." *I need to think. Without you.*

She felt like she'd been slapped. What was happening? They'd always been a team. Now he was shutting her out. "Do you want me to text the others?" she asked, trying to keep her voice from breaking.

"No! Just…no! Don't tell anyone!"

"They're going to find out anyway," she said. "We might as well get it over with."

"Just don't, okay? I don't want them talking about me. I don't even want them *thinking* about me."

"BJ, come on."

"I'm sorry. I love you. I'll call you later, okay?" He turned and walked away, leaving her standing in the lobby.

It was the first time he'd ever told her he needed time alone.

It was the first time he'd ever needed it.

"Thanks for meeting with me," Olivia said, fidgeting with her spoon. "I know we haven't hung out much lately, but I didn't know who else to talk to. You're the only one who would understand."

Olivia was smart, she was pretty, and she was nice. She had made lots of friends the past few years, but had basically put them all on the backburner for Cooper.

All of us liked her, of course. At least, we used to like her before her thoughts started to spiral again. Cooper, Mackenzie, Cooper, Mackenzie, NYU, Johns Hopkins.

"No problem," Tess said, her curiosity piqued. "What's up?" She tried to read Olivia's mind, but even now, all she got was Cooper this, and Cooper that. Cooper, Cooper, Cooper.

Olivia heard Tess's thoughts and blushed.

It was just before eight the next morning. They were in the almost-empty cafeteria, having juice and oatmeal. Tess picked up her juice, then put it back down. Picked it up again, put it down again. She looked at the door.

"Tess? You all right?"

She didn't answer.

"Oh. My. God," Olivia said, reading Tess's mind. "BJ lost his ESP?"

Tess frowned. "Don't say anything to him. He's upset."

"I won't. But won't he…" Olivia had been about to say, won't he find out that I know? But then she realized he wouldn't. How could he? "Another one down," she said grimly.

But why did it have to be him? Tess thought. *Why couldn't it be one of the others? Like Sadie, for instance. She couldn't care less.*

Or Levi, Olivia thought. *He just uses it to pick up girls. It would be good for womankind if he lost it.*

"We could be next," Tess said. "Any of us could."

Olivia shuddered. How would she know what Cooper was thinking?

"You could always ask him," Tess said.

Olivia shrugged. "He's not good with feelings." *At least not with me. He has no trouble telling his feelings to Mackenzie.*

Is that what this is about? Mackenzie and Cooper?

Olivia shrugged. *No. Yes.* She looked down at her oatmeal. "I just don't know what to do. Do I go for the better program or stay here and go to NYU to stay with Cooper?"

"Why are you asking *me*?"

"Well…" *Everyone else thinks it a bad idea! But you're the only one who would understand! You're going to school with your boyfriend!*

"It's not the same thing. We've been together for ever."

Olivia picked at her thumb. "What, so you guys are more likely to make it?"

Yes, Tess thought. She thought about last night. *Maybe.* She shook her head. "It's not just that. We both wanted to go to Berkeley."

Lucky.

"So you never worry about what would happen if you broke up?" Olivia asked.

"No," Tess said. "Not really." At least, she never used to. "What does Cooper think?"

"That's the problem! I don't know!" Olivia cried. "I listen to him all the time and he never thinks about college!" *He never thinks about me, either.*

Never?

Okay, not never. But not enough. Olivia sighed. *I know what you're thinking. That he's not as in to me as I'm in to him, so I can't pick NYU.*

Tess raised an eyebrow. *I wasn't thinking that. But it sounds like you are.*

I don't know what to do! I can't leave him! But I can't stay! I don't want to make the wrong decision! What's the right thing to do? Tell me what to do!

Tess leaned closer. "I can't! I don't know!"

Olivia fell back in her chair.

"So how often do you listen in on Cooper, exactly?"

Olivia picked her thumbnail. "It's not like he doesn't know. He hears me think about it later."

"You're kind of one step away from being a stalker," Tess said. "You're obsessing a little, huh?"

Olivia put her head down on the table. "A little? I can't stop." *It's too much. The enhancement, Mackenzie, losing our powers, the choices. I can't take it. My brain hurts.*

"So stop obsessing!"

"I can't!" She looked up at Tess with red-rimmed eyes. "Do you think Mackenzie and Cooper are going to get back together? Tell me the truth."

Tess's voice softened. "Olivia, they're just friends. And right now he's worried about her, and she's worried about him, too. That's what friends do. They care. Sure, sometimes Mackenzie thinks about the past, but that's about it."

"But I heard them!" Olivia burst out. "They miss each other!" *He's probably thinking about her right now. Let me see. No. He's still asleep. What if he's dreaming about her? I wish I could see inside his dreams.*

"Olivia," Tess said forcefully. "You're acting crazy."

"I'm not crazy, I'm worried! Come on, be honest. Are you saying you never worry about BJ? Wasn't he joking about me being naked last night when he was with you?"

Olivia spied on her, too? The girl was really losing her mind. "We don't have that kind of relationship," Tess said, checking her phone. "I trust him completely." Although it would be nice if he called her back.

Do you want me to listen in on him?

"No! I'll see him soon." She sighed. "He knows we're meeting. He's going to be mad that you know."

"So don't tell him," Olivia said. "Tell him I didn't show up."

Tess's eyes widened. "You mean lie? I can't do that. I've never lied to him before, and I'm not going to start now." Her phone buzzed. *Finally*, she thought. Then, "Crap. He's here. I don't want him to see you. He'll know right away that you know."

"No, he won't," Olivia reminded her. "Not if you don't tell him."

"He's thought-deaf, Olivia, not stupid. He'll know you read my mind."

BJ walked in to the cafeteria, saw Olivia, and scowled. "I guess she knows," he said, slumping into the chair next to Tess.

"It sucks," Olivia said.

He glared at Tess. "Have you been talking about me the whole time?"

"No, I mean yes. I mean—"

"Yeah, whatever. Like you said, they're going to find out anyway."

"This is true," Olivia said, nodding. *He looks devastated.*

He's not handling this at all, Tess thought.

"Stop it!" BJ said. "I know you're thinking about me!"

Tess put her arm around him. "I can't help it if she heard me thinking, BJ. But we weren't saying anything, I promise."

And then she froze. *There it is. My first lie.*

Actually, her first lie was when she told him that everything would be all right. We all know what they say about lying.

It's a slippery slope.

Chapter Twenty-Two
A POCKETFUL OF POSIES

BJ had lost his telepathy and nobody had told Pi.

Nobody.

She'd walked into homeroom completely clueless and had to hear it from Courtney, who'd heard it from Sadie, who'd heard it from Tess.

What kind of bullshit was that?

"You were supposed to text me immediately!" she yelled at him, shoving her finger in his face.

"Well, that didn't take long," he said, dropping into his chair.

"Of course it didn't take long! There are no secrets!"

He shrugged. "It just happened last night. Get over yourself."

He's pissed.

So pissed.

Wouldn't you be?

"Is everyone talking about me?" he asked Tess.

She froze. "Um…"

"What are they saying?"

"Nothing important."

He scowled. "Maybe I should switch homerooms."

"Don't you dare switch homerooms!" Pi said. "Do you want everyone finding out we're losing our powers? Have your eyes turned back yet?"

It took about twenty-four hours for our eyes to return to normal.

"Do I look like I care?"

"I do!" Courtney exclaimed. "I have endorsement deals!"

He better wear colored contacts.

Jordana gasped. "I'll have to take finals!"

"I repeat," BJ said, "do I look like I care?"

"It doesn't matter," Pi said. "They'll never let him switch so close to graduation."

"Let him switch what?" asked Mr Jonas, who'd just entered the room.

"Toothbrushes," Levi said. "He has to switch toothbrushes."

Toothbrushes? Isaac thought. *Really?*

They're worried about toothbrushes? thought Mr Jonas. *You know what? I don't want to know. Who knows what goes on in their weird minds?* Then he remembered he wasn't wearing his sunglasses. He pushed them onto his face and started writing on the whiteboard.

We need to discuss this further, Pi thought. *Bring your lunches to the courtyard. We'll meet there just after 1 p.m.*

Can we meet at 1:20? Levi asked. *The pizza line is really long.*

So buy a yogurt instead.

I can't make it, Sadie thought. *I'm meeting Michael for lunch.*

DUMBO!

Stop calling him that!

Has he ever thought about getting his ears tacked?

"Guys?" BJ asked, looking from person to person. "What's happening?"

Tess jabbed him in the side. *Shh! Mr Jonas can hear you! He'll know you lost your ESP!* Then she remembered that BJ couldn't hear her or anyone else, which was why they were having this discussion in the first place.

Right, Pi thought. *The thought-deaf ones. I'll shoot them an email. They can come if they want. Not that it'll do them any good.*

Don't forget Mackenzie, Cooper thought. *She's at the hospital, but maybe she'll come back for the meeting.*

Mackenzie, Mackenzie, Mackenzie, thought Olivia.

Cooper shot her a look.

Pi sent a group text:

```
Meeting in the courtyard at lunch.
```

She looked up at Sadie, then added:

```
Mandatory. Dumbo will have to wait.
```

* * *

"Please remove your sunglasses," Pi said to Edward. "You know the rules. No sunglasses among Espies."

"Since when?" he asked.

"Since now," she answered.

"But it's bright out here!" he complained.

And it was. It was a beautiful sunny day in May. Birds were chirping, trees were budding, the sky was clear.

And we were miserable. Another Espie was down. We wondered who would be next.

We were sitting in a circle in the courtyard behind the school. All around us, people were staring.

They're having a séance, someone thought.

Maybe it's a witches' coven, thought someone else.

Let's get the hell out of here!

In seconds, the courtyard was cleared of all non-Espies.

"They act like we have the plague," Edward said.

"We kind of do," Brinn mumbled. "We're all falling down, like in that nursery rhyme, 'Ring Around the Rosie'? It's about the Black Death. 'Ashes, ashes, we all fall down.'"

We all stared at her. *She's so weird*, Courtney thought.

I hope it's not contagious.

Being weird?

No, moron. Losing our ESP.

Olivia's heart was racing. *I don't want to be next, I don't want to be next, I don't want to be next...* She tried to swallow, but her throat was blocked. She felt sick to her stomach. *I can't deal with that. I just can't.*

"Olivia, are you okay?" Tess asked.

She doesn't look okay.

She looks like she's going to pass out.

Remember when she passed out in speech class?

"She did?" Mona asked.

"The first day she got telepathy," Mars said.

"Maybe she's doing it in reverse," Isaac said. "Maybe she's going to pass out and then lose it."

Noooooooo! "I'm not losing it!" Olivia cried. "I'm not!"

"She needs some air," Levi said.

"We're outside," Tess said, rolling her eyes.

Olivia took a few calming breaths. "Maybe it's time we went to Dr Dail." *Yes. That's what we have to do. We can't just sit around and wait for it to go.*

Pi frowned. "We've already been through this. We're not telling anyone."

"You told Jon," Courtney reminded her.

"That was different. He's a friend."

Really? When's the last time you spoke to him?

That romance sure got nipped in the bud.

Pi turned bright red.

Oh, look! She blushes! She's human!

"Maybe you should talk to him again," Sadie suggested. "We need help. What harm could it do?"

"We can do this on our own." Pi said, her voice tight. "Forget about Jon."

She should call him. They'd make a good couple.

Their kids would be little Einsteins.

Dorky little Einsteins.

Pi couldn't help herself. *He's not a dork. He plays guitar!*
She so likes him.

Cheeks on fire, Pi decided to change the subject. "Where is everyone? Didn't I say this meeting was mandatory?"

"Mackenzie's still at the hospital," Tess said. "She texted me to say she's not coming."

How is she? Cooper thought. *How's her mom?*

Her mother's doing great. But Mackenzie is still worried, of course.

Is she still hanging out with that guy? Isaac wondered. *Bennett? He was cute.*

He's a douche, Cooper thought.

Olivia scowled. "Can we please stay on topic?"

Wow. She's really worried about Mackenzie and Cooper.

I can't believe she talked to Tess about it ... What does Mackenzie think? ... I think she wants him back ... I think he wants HER back ... Who?... Mackenzie! ... Poor Olivia ... She's really stressed ... I bet she faints...

Olivia started humming loudly.

"I don't like Mackenzie!" Cooper yelled.

Well, this isn't awkward, Tess thought.

"I'm here!" Jordana called out, waving her freshly painted nails and running towards them. "Did I miss anything?"

Courtney had thought-commanded her to go back for a bottle of water. These days, she commanded her to do a lot of things, like tidying Courtney's locker, or doing her homework. Apparently, the weaker-minded the person, the more susceptible she was to suggestion. Half the time, Jordana walked around looking like a zombie. And the best part was that she didn't remember a thing.

Most of us were disgusted.

The twins wanted to switch into Courtney's group.

"We haven't started yet," Pi told Jordana. "Sit down."

Sit over by the tree, Courtney ordered. *Oh, and give me my water.*

Jordana sat down next to the tall oak tree. Then she got up again to give Courtney the bottle. Then she just stood there, blinking.

"Where's BJ?" Isaac asked. *Tess, is he not coming?*

"I don't know," Tess said. "He keeps changing his mind." *He's barely spoken to me all morning.*

"I'm here, I'm here," he said, just now coming into the courtyard. *Don't ask me why. Anojah and Nick didn't come. Why am I even bothering?*

Beats me, Pi thought.

"Because you want your ESP back," Tess said, trying to sound cheerful. *And I want the old BJ back.*

Typical. He can't stand it that his girlfriend is stronger than he is.

That's not it at all. ESP was their thing. Now their relationship is based on nothing.

What about sex?

They did have a lot of sex.

Now it's all they'll have.

Tess glared. *Can you guys shut the hell up?*

BJ looked around. "I suppose they're all talking about me."

"We're not talking about you," Mona said. "We're talking about your relationship with Tess."

"Super," he deadpanned.

Rather than squeezing next to Tess, BJ sat down next to Cooper. On BJ's left, Brinn was eating a banana.

Tess's heart sank. *He won't even sit next to me. Why is he acting like this? It's not my fault he lost his ESP!*

"Okay, then," Pi said. "Let's get started." She took out her iPad. "Everyone taking DHA please raise your hand."

What, this again? Tess thought.

Seriously? Mars thought.

Whatever, BJ thought.

The three of them raised their hands.

Pi nodded. "Like we discussed, whenever someone loses their ESP, the rest of the group will be absorbed somewhere else since we know whatever you're taking won't save your telepathy. Mars and Tess, you will stop taking the DHA immediately. You'll take something else, instead. BJ, you can do whatever you want."

"Can I take lutein?" Mars asked. *I want to be with Mona!*

"Don't take lutein," Mona said, suddenly panicked. *He can't take it!*

"Why not?" Mars asked suspiciously.

"Um, it turns your pee orange?" *Yup, yup, orange, orange, orange.*

It does not turn your pee orange, Isaac thought. *My pee is yellow. You've been eating too many carrots.*

Mona groaned. *Great. He's going to start monitoring me nonstop.*

Mars looked deflated. *I thought you wanted us to be together.*

I do! Just not all the time.

I promise I won't listen in on you. But I still want to do long distance.

"All right, then," Pi said, making a note in her iPad. "Mars, you're now in Group 3."

Yes! he thought.

Mona bit her lower lip. *This is going to be an issue.*

"What about you, Tess?" Pi asked.

Our group is the most fun, Isaac thought. *Pick us! Pick us!*

If she really loved me, BJ thought, *she'd take the antidote and give it up entirely.*

Tess nearly choked on her egg salad. *He wants me to give it up? He can't be serious. Can he?*

She looked at his angry face. "Put me wherever you want," she told Pi. "It makes no difference to me." *Can you put me in Group 6? That's the brain one where you get to plant suggestions, right? Maybe I can push some sense into BJ.*

"Got it," Pi said, making another note.

"I can't believe you thought that!" BJ exclaimed. "You are so two-faced!"

Tess gasped. *How...?*

Cooper sighed. "Sorry. I think I relayed what you thought."

"Look, just stop thinking about me, okay?" BJ practically yelled.

"I'm not!" Tess retorted.

They all are, Cooper thought. *Oops. I did it again.*

"What about you, BJ?" Pi asked. "Care to try something else?" *Nothing can help him now.*

"I'll just stick with the wine, thank you very much."

"Well, I guess that does it," Pi said, putting down her iPad. "I'll email everyone with the updated spreadsheet. Things should get back to normal."

We all snorted. Normal?

Olivia was disintegrating, BJ was furious at Tess, Mona was mad at Mars, and Courtney had become a dictator.

Plus, we'd lost another Espie.

Ashes, ashes, we all fall down.

Chapter Twenty-Three
LOVE BITES

Mackenzie hadn't checked her phone for hours. After she left her mother's room and went to the hospital's solarium, she discovered she had two messages. The first was from Pi with a new spreadsheet:

Group 1	Group 2	Group 3	Group 4	~~Group 5~~	Group 6
EARS	**EARS**	**EYES**	**EYES**	**BRAIN**	**BRAIN**
hear thru walls	relay	long distance	dud	~~dud~~	push thoughts
Magnesium	**Gingko**	**Lutein**	**Zeaxanthin**	~~**DHA**~~	**Cognizin citicoline**
Mackenzie	Cooper	Isaac	Pi	*defunct	Michelle
Brinn	Daniel	Olivia	Sadie		Courtney
Edward	Dave	Mona	*Jordana (no ESP)		Levi
		Mars			Tess

She thought about what it would be like to lose her ESP. Truth was, sometimes telepathy seemed a lot more trouble than it was worth.

Yesterday had been amazing when her mother woke up. She still had the tracheostomy tube, so she couldn't speak, and she'd been groggy and a bit disoriented from all the medication, but she was going to be fine. Mackenzie felt like a weight had been taken off her shoulders.

But then she heard her mother think, *I should write a new will. I want him to remarry if I die.*

"Mom, you don't need to make a new will," Mackenzie said, choking up. "And he's not getting remarried. Do you think I want a stepmother? Are you crazy?"

Her mother glared at Mackenzie and then started sputtering for breath.

Cailin gasped. "Omigod! Mackenzie! Shut up! Stop listening to her! She doesn't like it!"

"I'm sorry, Mom! I'm sorry! I won't listen! I promise!"

She's such a screw-up, Cailin thought.

Her mother started breathing normally, but then made sure her eyes were mostly closed whenever Mackenzie was in the room.

Which is why Mackenzie had started hanging out in the solarium.

The second message on her phone was from Bennett:

What are you doing tonight?

She sent a reply:

```
Mackenzie: At the hospital
Bennett: Tomorrow?
```

She felt a little irritated. Her mother had just had surgery, and he hadn't even asked how she was. Could he not be a tad more sensitive?

He sure seemed eager. Funny how the tables had turned. She'd worshipped him when she was a freshman, but he'd always blown her off. In spite of herself, she smiled. Now he was the one doing the chasing. She wasn't really into him, after everything she'd heard him think but...

She thought about Cooper. He'd made it clear that he was only interested in being friends. That the past was the past. She texted Bennett back:

```
Okay
```

Why not?

An hour later, she decided she was hungry and went down to the cafeteria for a quick bite. She spotted Olivia immediately, sitting at a table at the back. She was eating and checking her phone.

Mackenzie paid for her sandwich, and went over there. "Hey," she said, sitting next to her. "What are you doing here? I thought you worked Mondays and Thursdays." She thought that's what Cooper had said.

"They called me in," Olivia said, her voice pinched. "They were short in triage. I wasn't doing anything, anyway." She felt a prickle of irritation. *Why does Cooper feel the need to talk about me to Mackenzie?*

Mackenzie blinked in surprise. *Why do you feel the need to talk about me to my best friend?* she shot back. She knew the answer, of course. Olivia was jealous.

Do we really have to do this? Olivia took a deep breath. It was one thing to spy on someone from afar. It was another thing to confront her face to face.

You started it. But just so you know, you're wrong about me and Cooper. We're not getting back together.

You would, though. If he forgave you. Olivia gazed out the window. Mackenzie stared down at her hands. Except for the cashier, they were alone in the cafeteria.

Olivia looked back at Mackenzie. *Well?*

Mackenzie shrugged. *But he doesn't forgive me. And he's with you.*

Terrific. Olivia felt sick.

You're not going to throw up, are you?

"No," Olivia said. *Am I going to throw up? I'd better not throw up right here in front of her. What if I have the flu? I'm so going to get the flu. I'll be home sick, and Mackenzie and Cooper will hang out together at school and fall in love again. Omigod, I'm losing it.*

I'm trying to move on. I'm seeing Bennett again.

But you don't care about him.

Mackenzie sighed. *I'm trying to.*

Olivia played with her sandwich. *I should get the flu shot. Pi doesn't know what she's talking about. This whole interaction thing is bogus. This flu is horrible and a vaccine won't hurt my ESP. Maybe it will even help my ESP. Then everything will be fine. I'll be fine, Cooper will be fine, we'll all be fine.*

"You're getting a flu shot?"

"I should. There's a new bug going around. The ER is swamped. It starts with a fever and you get a rash. It's horrible."

"Sounds like what my mom had. They had to postpone her operation."

Olivia stood up suddenly. *I need to do something.* "I'm going to get it."

"The shot? Now?"

"Yes. Do you want it?"

Mackenzie shuddered. "No. Is Cooper going to get it?"

"He's not meeting me here, if that's what you're asking. I'm meeting him later. To help him with that English paper."

"*The Age of Innocence* paper?"

"Yup." *The book you told him all about. Because it was soooo romantic.*

Mackenzie flushed. Maybe it was time to get back to her mom.

Olivia hung her head. *What is wrong with me? Why am I being so horrible?* "I'm sorry," she said. "Your mom just had surgery and I'm going on and on about the flu and I'm being a jealous bitch."

"It's okay," Mackenzie said. "We all have a lot going on." *I know you're stressed.*

"How is your mom? Is her trach tube still in?"

"Yes."

"At least she can still mentally communicate with you," Olivia reminded her.

"That didn't go over well," Mackenzie said, remembering. *She shut me out.* She was always shutting her out. "You do that, right? Listen in on the patients?"

"All the time," Olivia admitted. "I help out by reading the minds of patients who for various reasons can't speak – mouth trauma, stroke, et cetera. Sometimes they freak out, but most of them appreciate it. The nurses and doctors definitely appreciate it."

"Well, my mother definitely doesn't appreciate it," Mackenzie said.

"Try again," Olivia repeated. "You can't give up on someone you love." *Which means I can't give up on Cooper.*

After Olivia went back to her floor, Mackenzie went to her mother's room, but she was asleep.

She went back to the solarium. She needed to write her essay, too. Or not. She couldn't concentrate. She kept thinking about what Olivia had said.

You can't give up on someone you love.

She's a good person, Mackenzie thought with more than a little regret. *I hope she makes him happy.*

Olivia was supposed to see Cooper later, but she wasn't sure where. That was so Cooper. He rarely made plans. No dinner reservations, or advanced tickets to movies or plays. All she knew was that they were supposed to work on his English lit paper. Was he coming over, or was she going there?

She'd texted him earlier:

Should I come over?

He didn't answer.

She listened in on him and heard, *Right! Left! Harder! I'm hungry.*

Right. He was playing video games.

At eight o'clock he finally texted:

Come over.

Okay then.

At his apartment, she found Nick, Levi, Edward, and Cooper squeezed on the couch playing Xbox. She wasn't exactly surprised.

It wasn't his fault his apartment was like their clubhouse. Or that Cooper was funny and sweet, the type of guy everyone wanted to hang out with. She just wished he'd spend more time with *her*. At least he was hanging out with the guys, though, and not his ex-girlfriend.

"What's up, Liv?" Nick said, his eyes on the TV. "How's life on the outside?"

"How long have you guys been here?" Olivia asked, opening a window. The place reeked of burnt popcorn and pot.

Days, maybe.

Months, even.

Not long enough.

"That's it for me," Levi said, dropping his controller. "I'm dead."

Olivia just stood there. She wasn't sure what to do.

"Come sit down," Cooper said.

Where? she wondered. She looked around the room. The armchair and loveseat were covered with laundry, and the couch was occupied. Greasy pizza boxes were piled at the door, and there were empty beer cans everywhere. Obviously, his father was out of town again, and wasn't expected back anytime soon.

"On his lap," Edward said.

This was not how Olivia had envisioned helping Cooper with his paper.

"Nick has to leave in a minute," Cooper said, pressing something on his controller. "Boo-ya! Did you see that? I totally massacred that creep!"

"How are you, Nick?" Olivia asked. "How's life without ESP?" She already knew the answer, of course. But she felt she had to make conversation. She couldn't just stand there.

"I'm GREAT," he said.

"Great? Really?"

"Really."

"You don't miss it?" she asked.

"No."

"No?"

"What, miss all that noise in my head? Nah." He put down his controller. "I'm outta here."

"Where?"

"Out." *Late date.*

"With who?" Olivia asked.

He smiled. "Sometimes I forget you guys can still hear me."

Nick left, and Olivia sat down on the couch.

Cooper kissed her quickly on the lips. *Do you care that they're here?*

No, she forced herself to think. *It's fine.*

It sounds like maybe you do.

I don't. But they're always here. And I want to talk to you about next year.

What about next year? He didn't take his eyes off the TV.

Was he serious? *About what you think I should do! College! NYU! Johns Hopkins!*

Whatever you want to do.

What does that mean?

Maybe we should go, Levi thought.

I'm winning here! Edward thought.

"We're supposed to work on your paper," Olivia said.

Who cares about papers?

Not me. We already got into college.

"I care about papers! And college!" Olivia screamed. "And I need to talk to Cooper! In private!"

There was silence.

She's going crazy.

Let's get out of here.

Cooper put down his controller. "Bye, guys. I'll see you later."

Two minutes later they were all out the door.

Cooper put his arm around her. "What are you so worried about?"

"I don't know what to do about school! I don't want to stay here if you're going to break up with me! But I don't want to leave you! But Johns Hopkins has a better program! But you're here! I don't know what to do! And you're not helping me make a decision! I need to make a decision! I can't make a decision!"

He put his hand on her knee. "Stay," he said simply.

"Stay?" she repeated.

"Stay," he said. *I want you to stay.*

Okay then. She took a deep breath. She would stay.

"Is anything going on with you guys?" Dr Dail asked after Lab. She had asked Pi to stay a moment. *You're all being weirdos.* She wasn't wearing her sunglasses.

"What do you mean?" Pi asked, trying to appear calm.

"I don't know," Dr Dail said. "You all seem...distracted." *They keep talking amongst themselves! I don't like it!*

"Yes, well. We're graduating. There's a lot going on. We have that cruise coming up, and then prom." Plus, she had just discovered that Olivia had gotten her flu shot despite Pi's warning. What nerve.

Part of her was disappointed Olivia hadn't lost her ESP, just so Pi would have been proven right.

Dr Dail nodded. "Right. You're graduating. Okay then."

She should have fun now before she becomes persona non grata.
I hope she makes it.

Make it? As a spy? Oh, she was going to make it. She was definitely going to make it.

Since it was lunch, Pi found herself wandering around the school. Then lingering outside the music room on the third floor.

She didn't really want to talk to Jon, but she couldn't help it if the door suddenly flew open and there he was, in full view. It would be rude not to at least say hello, right?

Naturally, the door didn't fly open.

Too bad there wasn't a supplement for telekinesis.

Maybe she should start taking cognizin citicoline *and* magnesium. She could push a suggestion right through the wall.

Mars's long distance kicked in on Friday. He started hearing Mona everywhere. He couldn't help it. He thought about her all the time. In his room. In the kitchen. Even in the bathroom. But then he'd realize she wasn't thinking of him, so he'd call her. "Why aren't you thinking about me?" he'd say. "Are you avoiding me?"

She started wearing sunglasses. And turned off her phone.

It was Saturday night, and Tess's mother was out on a date. Yes, a date. Her first one since Tess's father had moved out. She almost didn't make it out of the house.

Should I wear the red dress or the blue one? Should I just
wear pants? What will we talk about? What if he's a psychopath?

What if he's married?

Finally, the buzzer rang, and she was gone.

Five minutes later, BJ was in Tess's bed.

"I'm sorry," he was saying, looking long-faced. "I've been acting like an idiot."

"Yes, you have," Tess said. "You still want me to give up my ESP?"

"I just wish we could be the same. But, no, I want you to be happy." *Just because I lost mine doesn't mean she should, too. This doesn't have to change things.*

She didn't reply. Why didn't he sound convinced? Even his thoughts sounded forced. She couldn't help but feel suspicious.

"Tess?" he said, as though trying to read her mind. "We can make this work. We have to."

She sighed. "Come here," she said, pulling him toward her. At least he was trying. He was still the same BJ, only minus the ESP.

"Wait," he said, pushing himself up onto his elbow.

"What?"

"I...can you wear sunglasses?"

"You want me to wear sunglasses," she repeated. "While we have sex."

"Yes."

"No."

"Tess, come on."

"Why?"

"Why do you think?"

"So I won't hear your thoughts," she said.

"Ding, ding, ding," he said.

"You don't have to be mean about it."

"I'm sorry. I didn't mean to be mean. I just think it would be fair if you wore them. So we're on equal footing."

"We're not on foot," she joked, trying to lighten the mood. He didn't laugh.

She sighed again. "I'll keep my eyes closed," she suggested.

"They're open right now."

She slammed them shut. "There. Now are we good?"

"Come on, Tess."

She tried to kiss him, but his lips weren't there. She opened her eyes.

"See? You peeked! That's why you have to wear sunglasses."

"Fine, I'll wear sunglasses. Then will you be happy?"

"Yes."

"One sec." She got out of the bed and rummaged through her purse. She found them at the bottom. They were filthy, but whatever. She put them on and climbed back into bed. "Okay! They're on. Come here, big boy."

She tried to kiss him again, but the sunglasses banged into his nose. "Perfect," she said. "Nothing says sexy like a smashed-up nose."

"Less talking, more kissing," he said.

His hands were up her shirt, but she wasn't really paying attention. She was thinking about how annoyed she was. He didn't mind her having ESP – as long as she couldn't hear him. What kind of garbage was that?

Maybe he really did want her to lose her ESP. Which was

kind of selfish. Was that love? Shouldn't he want her to be awesome? What about the future? What if they got married? Would he be the type of husband who wanted his wife to succeed or the type to hold her back? She'd always thought he'd want her to shine. To publish her books. To be in the limelight. What if she was wrong? What if he wasn't the person she thought he was?

"I love you," he said, kissing her neck.

"I love you, too," she replied automatically, but she wasn't feeling it.

She pulled away from him and sat up. "I can't wear these," she said, taking off the glasses. "I feel like you don't trust me. Like you're trying to hide from me."

At first he just stared at her. His eyes looked sad. "Fine," he said, getting out of bed. He reached for his clothes on the chair. "But just remember, trust is a two-way street." He paused. "You know, maybe we should take a break."

She gasped. What? Was he kidding? "You want to break up with me?"

"I didn't say that. All I meant was that we should take some time to figure things out."

"How much time?" she asked, her shoulders stiffening.

He didn't answer, at least not out loud. *It probably won't be long before she loses her ESP. I just have to wait it out.*

"So you do want me to lose it." Her heart dropped.

"And this is exactly why!" he exploded. "I get why you were mad when I asked you to give it up, but you can't blame me for my private thoughts. But, yeah, I'm hoping it will go away all on its own. This one-sided thing sucks."

You will forget that notion immediately, she thought, fighting back tears. *You want me to keep my ESP. You want me to be successful. You want me to be happy.*

He looked at her as though puzzled, and then started getting dressed.

Either her new enhancement hadn't kicked in, or he was too strong-minded.

Pi had said you can't make people do things they don't want to do.

Tess suspected the latter.

Chapter Twenty-Four

ONE FLU OVER THE CUCKOO'S NEST

After Mackenzie's mother's trach tube came out, her brother left but her sister stayed in town, "I'll be with Mom this weekend," her sister said. "You'd better catch up on schoolwork. You can't fail. They'll rescind your Stanford acceptance. It's not a joke."

Mackenzie wanted to punch her. It made no sense. Mackenzie had telepathy. Their mother still couldn't speak. Yet they refused to let her help.

Please, honey, I don't want you listening. I'm depressed and I don't want you to hear, her mother thought. She blew a kiss and waved goodbye.

Her father shrugged. *Sorry, sweetie. She seems to want you to go.*

"She can still write," Cailin said. "It's not like she can't communicate. Don't upset her." *She doesn't need to worry about you right now.*

So Mackenzie went out with Bennett instead.

He was the one to notice her upper arm. It was covered in red and yellow blisters. It was disgusting.

"What is that?" he asked, sitting back.

It was the flu.

On Tuesday, Edward's skin started to tingle.

Was it finally happening? First, he had gotten telepathy, then he'd been able to hear through walls, and now he was going to start to sparkle… Was he finally turning into a vampire?

Nope. Flu.

By Wednesday, we were all out with the flu, even Mr Jonas.

Everyone but Olivia.

She'd had the shot and was the only one left in class.

I feel like a babysitter, thought the substitute teacher. *There's only one kid here.* She opened her iPad and downloaded a movie.

This is lame, Olivia decided. She told the sub she wasn't feeling well and went to Cooper's. He was alone in the apartment, and she was worried.

Of course she was worried. These days she was always worried.

She found him laid out in bed, feverish and covered in the rash. "Maybe you should go to your mom's. You really shouldn't be alone."

"I'm not alone," he murmured, and closed his eyes. "I have you. My personal guardian angel." He sang the last part.

Olivia couldn't help but smile. He was adorable, even when he was sick.

"Cooper?" she asked, when the singing stopped.

No answer. He was fast asleep.

Well, at least he wasn't high.

That night, Tess's push enhancement finally kicked in. She was lying in bed, her head feeling like it wanted to explode, when her mother appeared in the doorway. "Can I get you anything?" her mother asked. "A cold compress? A nice cup of tea?"

You know what? Tess thought, too weak to speak out loud. *Get me a shot of brandy.*

Two minutes later, her mom placed a shot glass on her nightstand.

On Thursday, Mars tried to monitor Mona from his bed, but he couldn't pick up anything. Either she was asleep or she was still wearing sunglasses.

He got a text from Isaac:

```
Sunglasses. For sure. Give her some
space!
```

Mars thought back: *Quit spying!*

It takes one to know one, Isaac mentally retorted. *Besides, I'm sick and bored. Do you think I should dye my hair?*

Courtney and Jordana were thankful that they'd already filmed the season finale. Nausea and cold sweats aside, all the makeup at Bloomingdale's couldn't hide their rash.

The good news: their show had been renewed for another season! Wahoo!

And so what if she lost her ESP? It hadn't hurt Jordana's role at all.

Who knew? Reality TV could be totally fake!

"I can't take it anymore!" Dave called up from the bunk below his brother. "You'd think that all this gingko would have protected us."

They'd been in bed for five days, and were obviously bored stupid. "That makes no sense," Daniel replied. "If gingko prevented people from getting the flu, why would there be flu shots?"

"Do we have any cough medicine? What about cream for the rash?" Dave asked.

That was the big question. Dave sent a group text:

```
Should we or should we not take
medication for our symptoms? What
about potential interactions?
```

Those of us who could hold our heads up texted back. The decision was unanimous: we could live with the cough, but the rash had to go.

* * *

The flu raged on for several more days, and then finally it was over. By Wednesday things were back to normal. Well, almost normal. BJ still wasn't talking to Tess, and Mackenzie's mother wasn't talking at all. Not that Mackenzie had been allowed anywhere near her mother's room, thanks to her flu. Even though her mother was probably immune, they didn't want her to infect the rest of the floor.

And then the bomb dropped and chaos resumed.

That night, we all got three texts:

```
Mona: It's gone.
Mars: I can't hear anything!
Isaac: Shit, shit, shit.
```

This round started with Mars. He'd been trying to listen in on Mona, but she was still blocking him. Why was she doing this to him? She loved him, didn't she? Was this how people in love behaved? He went to the kitchen to get some pickles. Some people ate chocolate, others ate ice cream…he ate pickles.

His mother knew about the pickles, so she knew he was depressed. His whole family had a thing for pickles, which was why the fridge was full of them.

Since she wasn't saying anything, he was expecting her to at least think, *What's wrong, sweetheart? Having a bad day?* But nothing. Not even a mental sigh.

Just a dull ache at the back of his head, which he attributed to the flu.

But it wasn't the flu. How could it be the flu? The flu was over. And so was his ESP.

Mona had been feeling guilty about the way she'd been treating Mars. Sure, he could be a little too in your face – in your whole head, actually – but he loved her and would do anything for her. Like making his sister bring her fresh chicken soup from Zuckers. Mona's mother always served it right from the can.

She homed in on his thoughts, but got nothing.

So she tried it on her mother.

Zilch.

"Mom!" she screamed. "Oh my god! Mom!"

Her mother came rushing into her room. "What is it?" she asked, alarmed. She'd been changing into sweatpants when Mona yelled, and had run into the room half-dressed.

"Think something!" Mona commanded.

"You scared me half to death because you need me to *think* something?"

"Yes!"

"Why?"

"Just do it!" A few seconds later: "I said do it!"

"I *am* thinking," her mother said. "I'm thinking that this is no way to talk to your mother."

Isaac had finally decided to dye the gray in his hair. He was still grieving over Richard and wanted to do something radical.

After he was done, he went into the living room to hear his older brother's opinion.

"So, Dar, what do you think?" he asked.

"Looks good," he said.

He waited to hear what his brother *really* thought.

But he heard nothing.

"Dar? What do you think?" he asked again.

"I told you. It looks good."

Still no thoughts. "Dar?" he repeated. "Darrrren!"

On Thursday, two days before the senior boat trip, we had plenty on our minds. Good thing Mr Jonas was late as usual.

Three more Espies were down.

"What the hell happened?" Mars asked, looking defeated. "All three of us were in the same group." He gave Olivia an accusatory look. "Why didn't *you* lose it?"

Yes, Olivia was in their group, and she was terrified.

Any minute, she could be ESP-less.

Her head felt kind of fuzzy, and her heart was thumping. *Omigod*, she thought. *It's happening now. Omigod, omigod, omigod—*

"Olivia, stop!" Pi ordered. Then her eyes lit up. *You are not losing your ESP. I've finally figured it out. The booster is in the flu shot.*

"I knew it was all about the booster!" Courtney cried.

"Omigod," Olivia said out loud. "It was the flu shot? Omigod, I've been saved!"

Ding, ding. Cooper's face lit up. "We should all get flu shots!"

Levi was confused. "Why? We already had the flu."

"Think about it," Pi said. "Do you really think it's a coincidence that everyone in that group except Olivia lost their ESP? I don't. I'm a scientist. I don't believe in coincidence. There's something in that flu shot that boosts the NFG. Something that was probably in the original shot, too."

"What about the interactions?" Mona asked. "What if something happens to us?"

A needle? Mackenzie thought. *Really? That's the solution? Can't we just take more pills?*

"It's worth the risk," Pi said. "And the sooner we do it, the better our chances. Besides, Olivia already had the shot, and she didn't freak out like Isabelle, did she?"

She kind of did, Tess thought.

"Not that kind of freak out," Pi said.

"I don't know…" Michelle said. "We should probably wait until after the cruise. They're announcing the prom court. What if we get another rash?"

We all shuddered.

Pi gestured impatiently. "We can't afford to wait. We just dropped three Espies. We could lose it any minute, too. Do you want to save your ESP or not?"

She's right. Besides, it's the flu that causes the rash, not the shot.

But what if we still get it?

What's a little rash if it means saving our ESP?

Do you remember the rash?

Someone asked me if I had leprosy!

Those of us who still had ESP nodded vigorously.

Those of us who didn't looked angry. Really, really angry.

"You're supposed to be a genius," Anojah snarled. "Well, thanks a lot, genius. Why couldn't you figure this out before?"

Pi ignored her. After all she'd done for them, they were giving her attitude? "So it's decided," she said. "After school today, we go and get flu shots."

"I guess this means the experiment is over," Tess said. "We can stop taking the supplements." Not that she minded. Pushing thoughts wasn't much use to her, anyway. Even if she could push some sense into BJ's head, she couldn't spend her life keeping him mesmerized.

Edward shook his head. "I'm not giving up my magnesium. I like listening through walls."

I'm not stopping, either. Jordana, give me your homework!

"Nobody is stopping anything," Pi said. "At least not yet. There's always a chance that the flu shot won't work. I suggest we give it a week. If no one else loses their ESP, we'll assume it's working. But, until then, the original plan stays in effect. Olivia, you need to switch to another group. What about gingko? Now you can be with Cooper."

"I'm staying where I am," Olivia replied. *Someone has to take care of him. This way, I can monitor him from a distance.*

"Hey!" Cooper said. On the one hand, he thought it was sweet how much she worried about him. On the other hand, he was beginning to feel a little...

Hemmed in?

Hemmed in?! I'm trying to take care of him!

I don't feel hemmed in. I don't. I like that you take care of me. I don't deserve you.

He really doesn't.

Olivia crossed her arms in front of her chest. "I'm putting my bets on the flu shot, anyway."

"Whatever," Pi said. "It's your funeral." Though the truth was, she was pretty sure it was going to work, too.

It had to.

What kind of genius would she be if it didn't?

Chapter Twenty-Five

CRUISING ALONG

With five decks, a heated pool, a tennis court and an elevator, the *City Queen* was massive. A ship its size could safely hide a person if that person didn't want to be found.

Cooper knew there would be two other schools there, but he had no idea that one of those schools would be Kennedy High. No idea that his friends from Jersey, the guys he'd cheated at poker, would be here on the ship.

Until he saw Alan.

He and Olivia were exploring the ship. Cooper spotted him the moment he and Olivia passed by the game room. Alan was leaning over the pool table, cue stick in hand, about to sink an eight ball.

That's one of the Jersey guys, Cooper thought.

What Jersey guys? Olivia thought back.

The ones I used to play poker with.

Here?

Yeah.

Olivia stared at him. He didn't seem to realize that this was a problem. She knew he had gotten high before setting sail. She grabbed his arm and hurried towards the exit. "We can't stay here," she said, once they were outside. "They're going to realize you're an Espie and they're going to want to beat the crap out of you. You've been stealing from them for months! They're going to hurt you, Cooper! We have to hide! We're out in the open. Come on, let's go!"

Oh. Right. "Where should we go?" he asked, looking around. They were on the top deck.

"The dining room. No, the nightclub. No, wait. The kids' center." Her heart was beating out of control. She needed to think. She had to protect him even if he couldn't protect himself. "No. We're all high school students on board. The kids center will be locked. The gym? The gym! That guy didn't look like he would visit a gym. Come on, let's go!"

"I am not hiding in a gym," he said.

She stared at him in disbelief. "You want to get beaten up? Or thrown overboard? Don't tell me they're above throwing you overboard."

"I don't think they'd go that far but… I can't say for sure." He sighed. "We can't hide the whole day. It's so nice out."

"Let's go, Cooper. Now." When he hesitated, she couldn't help but wonder if he wanted to get thrown overboard. Didn't he care at all?

"I care," he said. "Let's go."

The truth was, this cruise was one of the few things that Cooper had actually been looking forward to. He'd gotten stoned first, of course, but that would only make it more enjoyable. They'd left from the South Street Seaport, as they had breakfast by the pool. Now the ship was to sail around Manhattan and pass all the sites like the Empire State Building, the Freedom Tower, and the Statue of Liberty. It would end with a midnight buffet. Not that he hadn't seen it all before, but he liked the idea of seeing everything from the river.

Olivia had been worried before they even stepped on the boat. Sure, she imagined herself standing at the bow, Cooper's arms around her waist as she gazed out over the water, watching the city go by. Except she got that idea from the movie *Titanic*, and we all know what happened after the romantic part.

Yeah. It sunk.

Which, she imagined, could totally happen to this boat, too. There were no icebergs in the Hudson, but who knew what other crap lay in the water? People used the river as a garbage dump. *What if we hit something? What if the captain falls asleep and drives into a pier? What if we have to evacuate? Does the ship have enough lifeboats?*

Or what if Cooper realized how romantic the boat was but it made him realize that it was really Mackenzie he was in love with? What if the ship went down and there was only enough room in the boat for two and he took off with Mackenzie, leaving Olivia to drown?

What then?

She couldn't deal with all this.

And that was before she found out that there were people on board who might actually want to throw Cooper overboard.

She shook her head. They had to hide. Now.

After karaoke, there was a barbecue for lunch, followed by a trivia game on the lower promenade. It was now after three, and Mackenzie and Tess were sprawled out on deck chairs, soaking up the sun. Some of the guys were tossing a volleyball in the heated pool. It wasn't really a game, just a lot of splashing and horsing around.

Mackenzie was thinking about her mother. She was coming home from the hospital today. And Mackenzie wouldn't even be there. She had offered to skip the cruise, but her father had insisted she go.

"We want you to enjoy yourself," he said. "We'll be fine without you."

They never needed her. When Mackenzie went to see her mother, she could catch a thought or two, but that was it.

She should be in school.

I don't want her falling behind.

I don't want her worrying about me.

So she went to school.

And then after school she met up with Bennett.

What was she doing with Bennett? Did she even like Bennett? She wasn't sure. She liked his Harley. Maybe she should get her own.

"You'd look so hot on a Harley!" Levi called out from

the pool, reading her mind.

She was glad Bennett wasn't there. No outsiders were allowed, which meant no dates. Unless, of course, you were dating someone who was already going.

Like Tess and BJ, for instance. Except he was barely talking to her, and she was miserable. He'd told her he wanted time to figure things out, but she knew the truth. He was waiting for her to lose her ESP.

Waiting for her to fail.

Which was why he was miserable, too. It wasn't going to happen, now that they'd found a cure.

"The level of his dickishness has reached a new high," Tess was saying to Mackenzie. "Maybe I shouldn't have gotten the flu shot. What's more important? My relationship or my ESP?"

Mackenzie raised an eyebrow.

Tess flushed. "Yeah, I know. I'm turning into Olivia."

"He's just being stubborn," Mackenzie said. "He'll come around. Speaking of Olivia, there she is."

"Hi, guys," she said, eyes darting around the deck. "Have you seen them?"

"The Jersey guys? No," Tess said. "But I have no idea what they look like."

Olivia stood beside the empty deck chair next to Mackenzie. "Cooper is getting a little antsy. I told him I'd see where they were so maybe he could come out of hiding."

"Do you think you're being a bit crazy?" Tess asked. "Why don't you come sit down and relax a little?" Without sunglasses, Tess was squinting in the sunlight. We were all squinting, yet we refused to wear sunglasses. At least those of us who still had ESP.

"There's no time to relax!" she argued.

"Olivia, you need to take a deep breath. And Cooper is going to miss the whole cruise! Who cares if they see him! They might not realize that he's an Espie."

"Alan knows there are Espies on board," Olivia says. "You don't think I walked by him to see what he knew? Everyone knows there are Espies on board! What do you think they're going to do to Cooper if they realize what he's been up to?" She looked at Mackenzie for support. She still cared about him, so she must be worried about him, too. Wasn't she?

Mackenzie sighed. *I'm worried. I guess I didn't think it all through.*

Olivia rubbed her temples. *No one ever does! That's why I have to worry about everything!*

Tess shook her head. "Did he even eat lunch?"

"I brought him a hot dog," Olivia said.

"Hey, girls. Come swim!"

They looked up to see Teddy. Wearing orange swim shorts and Ray-Bans, he was standing at the foot of Tess's chair, dripping all over her beach bag.

"That sounds like an excellent idea," Tess said. She wasn't going to sit around moping all day just because BJ was being a baby.

She gave her friends a salute and cannonballed into the pool.

"I gotta go," Olivia said nervously.

"I gotta pee," said Mackenzie, and slipped on a cover-up.

* * *

Olivia had been gone for a half an hour and Cooper was bored. He was sick of watching the TV over the treadmill. He wanted to go outside. And he was still hungry. How dangerous could it be? He'd be lightning fast in the dining room and, besides, he had his hoodie.

He ran to the dining room. There! He'd done it. No one had seen him. Olivia was worrying for nothing.

There was ice cream! He picked up a bowl and got a scoop of chocolate. He was starving. Were there any cookies? He kind of had the munchies.

"Leo!" shouted a big beefy guy from the doorway. Cooper recognized him immediately. Alan. And he was headed Cooper's way.

So much for the anonymity of hoodies.

But big deal. So Alan saw him. That didn't mean he knew anything. He would just play it cool. He could do that. He always played it cool.

Alan was by his side, slapping him on his back. "How the hell are you?" he said. "Where have you been?"

"Around," Cooper said sheepishly. "You know how it is."

"We were just going to get a game going. You in?"

"Sorry," Cooper said. "I'm here with my girlfriend. She'd kick my ass." He noticed Olivia staring at him through the door.

Oh, no. She was going to freak.

He saw her approaching. Yup. Her thoughts were going bonkers.

Cooper! What are you doing? You're going to get caught! They're going to throw you overboard! You're going to drown! You're going to get eaten by sharks!

Cooper was pretty sure there were no sharks in the Hudson.

That is not the point! Olivia screamed.

It's going to be okay, Cooper thought back. *They haven't made the connection. I'm not going to play. You need to relax.*

Okay, she thought. *Breathe. Breathe. Breathe.* She seemed to be calming down.

"Wait a sec," Alan said, looking across the room. "Aren't they those reality chicks? You know, from that show?"

Jordana and Courtney had just entered the dining room.

Shit. Shit, shit, shit. "I'm not into reality," Cooper said. He started to sweat.

Olivia started to hyperventilate.

"Do you know them? They go to Bloomberg, right? They're so hot. I knew Bloomberg would be here. You don't go there, do you? I thought you're from the Bronx?" Alan's forehead creased in thought. "Unless you do go to Bloomberg?"

"Um…" What was he supposed to say? "I don't know them," was all he could think of. He had to get out of there. Fast.

Courtney had overheard that one of Cooper's gamblers was on deck during lunch, but unfortunately, Jordana had no idea what was going on and headed right for them.

Ah! No!

"Hi, guys," Jordana said, giving Alan the eye. "What's up?"

"Hello," Alan said, with a lazy smile. "We have celebrities on board."

"You certainly do," she said.

Sorry! Courtney thought. *This is the guy?*

Why didn't you tell her? Olivia barked, joining them.

Don't blame this on me, Courtney thought. *I'm not the degenerate gambler.*

I like the short one, Alan thought. "So what's it like?" he asked Jordana. "Is it true you can hear everything?"

"Everything," she said, flipping her hair.

"Even the dirty stuff?"

"Especially the dirty stuff."

He laughed. "Wanna go get a drink?"

"I thought you had a game," Cooper said quickly. This was bad. This was very, very bad.

He wouldn't like her better than me if he knew she'd lost her ESP, Courtney thought. Then to Jordana: *Tell Cooper's friend he's not your type.*

"I'm sorry, Cooper's friend, you're not my type," Jordana said, her eyes glazed over.

"Who's Cooper?" Alan asked.

Courtney! Olivia screamed.

Cooper's blood froze.

Courtney paled. *Oops.*

Oh no, oh no, oh no. "Cooper goes to our school," Olivia piped up, thinking fast. "But he's not one of us," she added, then turned red. "I mean, one of them. I mean, he's not here today."

Alan looked confused. "One of what? A psychic?"

"We're not psychics," Jordana said, twirling a lock of hair.

"We're artists. Of course, some of us are more talented than others. Though maybe *enhanced* is a better word."

Courtney, order Jordana to stop talking! Cooper thought, his pulse racing.

Fine with me. Who does she think she is anyway, acting like she still has ESP? Jordana, shut your mouth!

Olivia's eyes darted around the room with fear. *We need to get out of here! He's going to realize Leo is Cooper!*

Alan stared at Olivia. "Leo is Cooper?" he asked.

Oh my god! Olivia thought. She looked at Alan and then back at Cooper. *You're relaying! He can hear me through you!*

Cooper turned white and closed his eyes.

Olivia slammed her eyes shut too.

"Why did she call you Cooper?" Alan asked. "What the hell, Leo?"

"I...uh..."

"Tell me this guy's name," Alan said to Jordana.

"Cooper," she said through clenched lips.

Alan turned purple. "You scumbag," he spat, and grabbed Cooper by the collar. "You're one of those psychics! You're not Leo, you're Cooper, and you've been cheating me since day one!"

He grabbed Cooper by the neck.

"Help!" screamed Olivia. "Someone help!"

Where are the cameras when we need them? thought Courtney. *This would make great TV.*

But before Alan could plant his fist into Cooper's face, Teddy, who had come up from behind, grabbed his arm and wrestled him to the ground.

Alan broke free of the hold. "I'll stop!" He stood up and smoothed his rumpled shirt. "This isn't the end of it," he said, leering at Cooper. "You can bet on that." He muttered to himself as he skulked off.

Cooper was still shaking. "Thanks, Teddy."

"No problem. What was that about?"

"Poker debts," Olivia said.

"Oh!" Jordana squealed. "That was the guy you were cheating? Why didn't anyone tell me?"

"We tried," Courtney grumbled.

"You should never have left the gym," Olivia said.

Cooper laughed. He couldn't help it. "That was close."

"Are you kidding me?" Olivia screamed. "How do you think that made me feel? He was going to beat the crap out of you! I thought he was going to kill you! That was close? That was *close*?! What is wrong with you? Do you care about anything, Cooper? Anything at all?" She glared at him before storming off.

Pi was at the ice cream table when the fight broke out. She was planning to take a tray outside and then do some Sudoku.

Then she saw Jon.

"Why aren't you misbehaving with your friends?" he asked, picking up a bowl. He piled on three scoops of ice cream, followed by a glob of chocolate sauce.

Pi grimaced. "This isn't a circus. It's a cruise."

"Have you ever been on a trapeze?"

"No," Pi said. "Have you?"

"No. But I've always wanted to. Want to try with me?"

"Not really," she said. "I generally try to steer myself away from activities that could cause brain damage."

"Oh, come on," he said. "I'm going to dive the Great Barrier Reef."

"You're certified?"

"Not yet. I'm taking a course when I get to Australia."

She looked out at the water. She'd always been curious about diving. "Imagine seeing a shark."

"There's a whole world down there," he said. Then he pointed out with his chin. "There's a whole world out there, too. Sure you don't want to see it?"

"Oh, I'm going to see it," she said. "You think they're going to keep me locked in a room in D.C.?"

"Who knows what they'll do with you?" he said. "It won't be up to you, that's for sure. I like to be in charge of my destiny."

Pi bristled. She *was* in charge of her destiny, thank you very much.

"I don't want to fight with you," he said. "I'm leaving in less than a month." He took a step closer to her.

"What do you want then?" she asked. She could feel his breath against her cheek.

He smiled. "I want you to come to prom with me. I hear the band is great."

"What? Seriously?" She laughed. "You want to go with *me*?"

"Yes, I do." *I like you.*

"Why? I'm so not your type."

You said I needed a new type. And I'll probably never see you again. "Why not?"

Why not. Why not? "Okay," she said at last. "Why not."

Tess was making her own sundae when Teddy came up to her and said, "That fight made me hungry."

"Great wrestling," she said, beaming at him. "I heard you kicked some ass."

"I did," he said. "Come eat with me?"

She looked across the room. BJ was leaning against the wall, watching them. She decided to give him something to see. "Of course," she said to Teddy. She took his arm and let him lead her to a table.

"Seriously," she said, as they sat down, "I heard you were awesome."

"It was nothing," he said, but grinned just the same. *Tess is awesome. I'm going to miss her.* He was going to Arizona State.

"I'm going to miss you, too," she said. "But we'll be close-ish. We can visit you."

"We?" he said. "What's the deal with you and BJ?" *I heard you broke up.*

She looked down at the table. Had they? Or were they just taking some time off? "We're working on it," she said, with more conviction than she felt.

"Are you going to prom together?" he asked. "If not, wanna go with me? For old times' sake?" *She's not taking this the wrong way, is she? We just used to be such good friends and my mother loves her and I think it could be fun and then maybe I could still go home with Rayna even though she's going with Dave...*

Tess laughed. "As friends. Got it." She put her hand on Teddy's. "Let me see what happens with BJ."

"Now, isn't this sweet." His tone was drenched in sarcasm.

Tess looked up to see BJ glaring.

"We get into one fight and you run to good old Teddy?"

"We're friends, BJ," Tess said.

He's trying to screw her for sure.

"He's not," Tess said, putting her hands in her lap. For the millionth time, she wished he still had his ESP.

He covered his eyes with his hands. "Stop doing that!"

"Grow up!" she yelled. She stood up and grabbed his arm and led him onto the deck. "This is crazy," she said. "Teddy isn't trying to sleep with me, BJ. We're just friends. You know that."

"You used to like him," he said.

"And then there was you," she replied, putting her hand on his shoulder. "And I'm closer to you than I've ever been to anyone in my entire life."

"Yeah, but that's because of the telepathy!"

"It is not! We're not just about the telepathy!"

He shook his head. "You don't know what it's like to lose it."

She sighed. He was right. She didn't.

"Come back inside," she said, over a lump in her throat. "Let's talk about it. We can work this out. I know we can."

He shook his head. "No. We're not who we were. I can't take it. It's not you. It's..."

"You've got to be kidding me," she snapped, putting up her hand. "Don't you dare throw clichés at me!"

It's me, he thought. *I can't be around you. It hurts.*

"You're breaking up with me?" she whispered. "For real?"

I'm sorry, he thought. His eyes were wet. *But it's over.*

Chapter Twenty-Six
THE WAY WE WERE

"Hey," Cooper said.

Farther along the promenade, Mackenzie, lost in her own thoughts, had been looking out at the Hudson when Cooper came out of the dining room.

"Hey, yourself," she said, turning around. "Does Olivia know you're out of hiding?"

"She's kind of mad at me right now," he admitted.

"Something to do with the commotion inside?" She gestured toward the dining room.

"You heard it?" he asked, surprised. "It wasn't much of a commotion."

"I could hear it through the walls. But only some of it. There was too much emotion – no one was thinking very clearly." Then she paused. "She was right. You were being an idiot. You should find her."

He took a step closer. "Yeah, I know. I should do a lot of things."

"So he didn't hit you?" she asked, studying his face. "Looks like you're going to live."

"Oh, well," he said.

"Don't talk like that."

"Like what?"

"Like nothing matters."

His mouth turned down. "Nothing does. This cruise has been the only thing I've been looking forward to all month and I had to hide out in the gym. The gym is disgusting. It smells like BO."

"What about school? Aren't you excited about college?"

"Are you?" he shot back.

Not really, she admitted. *Everyone thinks I'm going to flunk out.*

You're not going to flunk out. You're smarter than they give you credit for.

Hah! I don't even know what I want to study. Maybe I should drop out and take some clothing design classes in New York. I like clothes.

"If you want to apply to FIT or something, that's one thing," he said. "But you're smart enough to do well at Stanford. This is your chance to prove it. You can take design classes when you get there."

"Trying to get rid of me?"

"Never," he said.

The sun was descending rapidly. In the distance, she could just make out the outline of another ship. *Two ships passing in the night,* she thought. *Kinda like us.*

His phone rang in his pocket, but he ignored it.

Olivia?

Probably.

You're not going to get it? A cool breeze blew in from the water, tousling her hair into her face.

No, he thought, as he smoothed the hair away.

I wish we could go back in time, she thought. They were standing so close, she could feel his breath.

Here, in the waning light, it was easy to imagine him as he once was. Easy to picture the Cooper of two years ago, with his carefree smile and warm, inviting eyes. Easy to remember the way things used to be.

I remember the way I felt about you, he thought. His heart raced. *The way I still feel about you.*

She held her breath. *What if we could start over?*

And then he kissed her.

And she didn't pull away.

At that moment, Principal Roth, holding a microphone and wearing sunglasses, was standing at the front of the dining room, announcing the nominees for Bloomberg High's prom king and queen.

Everyone was kind of shocked at the list.

It included Michelle, Olivia, Courtney, Pi, Jon, BJ, Henry Oregon, and Mike Sheppard. Since Principal Roth had chosen the list, he had chosen Jon, Pi, Olivia, Henry and Mike because they had the highest GPAs. He chose Michelle because she made him. But we couldn't figure out why he chose Courtney and BJ.

She's great in that reality show. And his nickname is hysterical, the principal thought. Mystery solved.

Olivia hadn't even heard her name being called. She was very busy worrying about Cooper. Why hadn't he answered the phone? Where was he? Was he avoiding her? Had Alan thrown him overboard? She tried homing in on his thoughts, but all she got was a pain in her head.

Something wasn't right. She couldn't even breathe. She had to get some air before she passed out.

"Congratulations!" people cheered, as she rushed past them.

At another table, Mars and Sadie were discussing their love lives over a plate of s'mores. Mars was depressed because Mona was a junior and couldn't be with him on the senior cruise, and Sadie had broken up with Dumbo. She decided she preferred his roommate. "You've got my vote!" she called out, as Olivia ran by.

"What? No way!" Michelle cried out. "Everyone's voting for me," she commanded. "Do you hear me? Everyone is voting for me! Do not try to ruin this for me, Courtney!"

Courtney flipped her hair. "I don't care about being stupid prom queen. I'm a TV star." *I totally want to be prom queen.*

At a third table, Brinn, wearing a sailor's cap and a life preserver, was peeling a banana. "I'm not voting for any of you," she mumbled.

Suddenly feeling dizzy, Olivia stopped moving. The dining room started spinning, so she leaned against the wall.

Something was happening. What was happening? Was she losing her ESP? No. No, no, no, no. She couldn't lose it, she needed it, she couldn't lose it. What would happen to her if she lost it? She would lose her mind, too.

"You look pale," she heard someone say over the ringing in her ears. "Are you that excited about being nominated? You're not going to faint, are you?"

"It's my head. Hurts...so...much..."

The next thing Olivia knew, she was lying flat on the dining room floor.

"Oh my god!" she heard Sadie screech. "Somebody help!"

"Is she all right?"

Olivia's eyes popped open.

"Is she drunk?"

"She probably had too much sun."

"Nah, she's always fainting."

"Where's Cooper?"

That was so embarrassing, she thought. *Everyone must think I'm a total freak*.

Except they weren't thinking at all. They were talking out loud.

It was like watching TV after someone had pulled out the plug. Or like listening to a phone you forgot to charge.

She couldn't hear a thing.

"I'll find Cooper," Edward said. He looked around the dining room, and when he didn't see Cooper, he listened through the walls. At first he didn't hear anything. But then –

Mmmmm...Mackenzie...

Oh! Oh, no.

"Where is he?" Olivia asked, her hands trembling. Her whole body was trembling. *It's gone, it's gone, it's gone.*

"Just outside on the deck," Edward said, not meeting her eyes. "I'll get him."

He ran up the stairs and found them. They were still lip-locked.

He coughed. Twice. "Hey, man," Edward said, embarrassed. "Sorry to interrupt, but we have a bit of a problem."

Edward quickly filled them in as Cooper pulled back. Cooper immediately felt like a total asshole. *What did I do? I am just as bad as my dad!*

Mackenzie snapped out of her trance, too. *How could I do that to Olivia?*

That was a mistake, Cooper thought, running to Olivia. *I am not that guy. I can't be that guy.*

By the time he reached the dining room, those of us who still had ESP all knew what had happened.

Some of us felt he should tell Olivia; others thought it would only hurt her.

She could no longer hear thoughts.

She would never know.

When Cooper saw Olivia, she was staring into space. She looked shell-shocked. He put his arms around her.

"It's okay," he told her.

"It's so quiet," she said slowly. *Everything is quiet.*

"I know," he said. *Maybe it's better this way.* "We'll be home soon. Everything is going to be okay."

It was quiet. So quiet. She couldn't hear what he was thinking. She couldn't hear what anyone was thinking.

He led her outside. She held on to the railing. She listened to the lapping sound of the water.

So quiet.

For the first time in months, Olivia felt calm.

Chapter Twenty-Seven
BACHELOR PAD

Mackenzie woke up early. She'd forgotten to close her blinds and the sun flooded in.

The memories flooded in, too.

What was wrong with her? How could she have done that to Olivia?

In sophomore year she'd been a cheat. Now she was a home-wrecker. Couldn't she do anything right?

I wish I was eating eggs, she heard from the other room. *Scrambled. With onion. And cheese. Sharp cheese.*

Was that her mom? Yes! Her mom was home!

They had taken the trach tube out, but her mom still couldn't speak.

Maybe, she realized standing up, there *was* something she could do.

Thirty minutes later, she had gone to Whole Foods, come back, and made her mom and dad brunch.

She opened her mom's door, put a loaded breakfast tray on the bureau, and sat on her bed. "You ordered scrambled eggs with onion and cheese?"

Her mother pulled her covers up to her chest. *You listened to me?*

"Yes," Mackenzie said. "I did. And I am going to keep listening to you. I want to help you."

Her mother shook her head. *No. You're my baby. It's my job to take care of you.*

"Stop treating me like I can't handle this!" Mackenzie said, her voice rising. "You're being ridiculous! You can't speak. I can read minds. This is a friggin' miracle, OK? Let me help you."

Mackenzie's mom closed her eyes and then opened them again. *What if the cancer comes back?*

"It won't."

It might.

"Then we'll fight it. Together."

Her mom looked at her. *I'm scared. I want to protect you. I've always wanted to protect you. But what if I can't?*

She climbed into bed beside her mom. "Then I'll protect us both. Have you noticed? I'm a freakin' superhero. Now eat."

Olivia was standing on Chambers Street when she saw Mackenzie go into Whole Foods. She tried to wave but was holding two cups of hot coffee. She called out, but Mackenzie didn't hear.

Two days ago, seeing Mackenzie would probably have sent her down a spiral. Was she thinking about Cooper? Did she still love him? Was she going to try to steal him?

But today Olivia just watched her go.

Olivia's mind was quiet. She'd forgotten what it felt like to have a quiet mind. She'd forgotten what it sounded like when the only voice in her head was her own.

She liked it.

She stopped at the corner and waited for the walk sign. She listened as the taxis, buses, and cars rushed by with a whoosh.

She didn't know what would happen with her and Cooper. How could she?

But she had made her decision and Johns Hopkins had given her scholarship to someone else.

Maybe going to NYU was the wrong choice. Maybe they'd break up. But maybe she'd fall in love with a stranger on the 6 train. There was no way to know if her decision – or any decision – was right or wrong, was there? Even if she made the *right* one, it's not like she could ever confirm it.

No. Sometimes, you just had to make a move.

The light changed. She looked both ways and crossed the street.

That afternoon, Dave and Daniel were playing hacky sack in the park. They had a whole routine.

I'm going left!
I'm going right!

Suddenly a sharp pain imploded in their heads and they couldn't hear anything.

"Nooooo!" they both wailed. "Our twin powers are gone!"

Later that evening, Cooper was watching the Yankee game when his father came into the room.

"Hey, Coop," his father asked. "Are you moving into the dorm next year?"

"I don't know," Cooper said. "Seems like kind of a waste of money. Since you live so close and you're never here."

"It might be good for you," his dad said. "Living on your own." But what he thought was, *Kara wants to move in.* He shrugged, realizing he'd given his real motive away.

Cooper didn't even know who Kara was. New girlfriend, he supposed.

"Right," Cooper said. "OK. I'll look into it. I may have missed the deadline to apply." He stared back at the TV. He had no idea if that was true.

"Oh," his dad said. "What's the score?"

"Five nothing, Yankees."

"Great," his dad said, and walked out of the living room.

Cooper didn't feel great. Actually, he felt like shit. His dad wanted to kick him out. Plus, he knew that what had happened with Mackenzie was a huge mistake. They'd both been feeling vulnerable. It was easy to get caught up in a moment when everything was a mess.

Who was he to judge his father? He was just as bad.

Even a Yankees win wouldn't cheer him up. Cooper was

miserable. Plus, he had a headache.

"You know what, Cooper?" his dad said, coming back into the room. "Maybe you should get your own place. I'd pay for it. A studio, maybe? Or a two-bed? You could move in with one of your friends. You'd love it. I'd miss having you here, but it would be a great experience for you."

Right. "Yeah, maybe. You know what? I'm gonna go for a walk."

Cooper walked to the river. Then he followed the path all the way to the top of the island.

He needed the fresh air. He needed to move his legs. He needed to move to a new place.

An hour later, he was cutting through the alley behind his building, thinking about how maybe everything would be okay. He could pull it off. He had Olivia. He'd find somewhere to live.

Then he heard a familiar voice.

"Hey, tough guy, going somewhere?"

It was Alan, and he wasn't alone. Two other guys had emerged from the shadows. He tried to run, but one of the other guys grabbed the back of his shirt.

"You live in a nice part of town, *Cooper*," Alan said. "Took us two hours to get here."

"How did you find me?" Cooper managed, over the thundering in his chest.

Alan laughed. "Seriously? How many psychics named Cooper do you think go to your school?" His face sobered. "Tell me something, asshole – why would someone with a shitload of dough go around screwing guys like us?"

They circled him like a pack of wolves, and Cooper's stomach dropped. All his senses were heightened, every detail amplified in his mind. The rustling wind, the chill of the night. The angry look on Alan's face as he raised his fist and punched him.

Again. And again.

His head hurt. A lot.

They took his phone and the money out of his wallet. "This is ours," Alan said.

"Hey! Hey!" screamed a doorman. "I'm calling the police!"

The guys ran.

From the ground, Cooper stared at the sky.

The doorman came rushing over. "How bad is it?" he asked.

"Not that bad," Cooper said. He tried to listen to what the doorman was thinking.

But he couldn't hear a thing.

"I have this theory," Nick said on Monday before class. "I think you get to keep your ESP for as long as you need it, and then it goes away. Take me, for example. I lost mine, and I feel great."

"That's beyond stupid," Dave said, and Daniel agreed. What about their telepathy act? What about Vegas? Without their ESP, they could kiss their show – and their showgirls – goodbye. They wanted their ESP back. Pronto.

Funny thing was, Cooper kind of agreed with Nick. He was doing fine. In fact, he was better than fine. He was feeling great. His ass had been kicked. That was done. He could move on with his life.

He could move on with Olivia.

She was doing great, too. Now that she'd lost her ESP, she didn't have to worry about it anymore. She wasn't picking her fingers. Cooper couldn't hear her thoughts, but the people who could said she wasn't obsessing.

Which was why we decided not to tell her about Mackenzie. We were afraid it would push her over the edge again.

"Well, I still need my ESP," Michelle said. "Courtney is trying to beat me in the prom queen race!" She glared across the horseshoe at Courtney. "I heard you pushing thoughts this morning! Don't think I didn't! I know what you're up to!"

"I wasn't pushing," Courtney snapped. "I was just making a suggestion. Olivia, you don't care if you lose, right? You don't really want to be prom queen?"

"Not at all," Olivia said, with a shrug. *Having a prom queen is dumb.*

"Well, I don't need my telepathy," Sadie said. "But I still have it. So I'm not sure I buy your theory, Nick."

"Don't you want to hear what Dumbo thinks about the fact that you're sleeping with his roommate?" Courtney asked.

"Not really," she said.

By the end of homeroom, Sadie was having horrible headaches.

By lunchtime, her ESP was gone.

And while she never knew for sure how Dumbo felt about her hooking up with his roommate, she guessed that he wasn't thrilled.

* * *

Pi sat in her room, staring out the window.

On a scale from 1 to 100, her confidence level was 3.14159. We were falling down like bowling pins, and there was nothing she could do to stop it. Her flu vaccine theory had been a total bust.

Of course, she realized, twirling a pen with her fingers, there was still a chance that the original experiment could work. It was a long shot, but a shot nonetheless. Pi had been in Sadie's group, so now she had to choose another supplement. There were two groups left: Mackenzie, Edward, and Brinn in Ears 1; Tess, Michelle, Courtney, and Levi in Brain 6. Naturally, she chose Brain and proceeded straight to the pharmacy for some cognizin citicoline. But then she thought, *What the heck*, and picked up some magnesium as well.

The next day in class, the remaining two groups realized what she was doing and decided to take both supplements, too.

If they were going out, they might as well go with a bang.

Chapter Twenty-Eight
PROMS AND PROMISES

Three more Espies went down on the day of prom.

Edward had been getting dressed when he heard his parents talking about him through their bedroom wall. Hoping they'd decided on a graduation gift, he tried to home in on their thoughts, but all he got was a pain in his head. He was about to knock on their door when suddenly it flew open.

The bad news was that it broke his nose.

The really bad news was that he'd lost his ESP.

The really, really bad news was that now he'd probably never become a vampire.

Levi hated his tux. "Tell me the truth," he said to his sister. "Do I look like a waiter?" She just smiled. Unfortunately for him, she lived by the motto, *If you can't say anything nice, don't say anything at all*. He tried to read her mind, but he couldn't get any information there, either. Bye, bye, ESP.

Brinn broke the news to us at prom, but wouldn't give us details. Wearing a black slinky gown, she was actually dressed normally for a change. Except for the cape. Which kind of made her look like a bat.

Edward thought she looked cute.

She was also wearing wing-tipped sunglasses. "If I can't hear you," she said, "why should you hear me?"

Which meant only five of us were left: Mackenzie, Pi, Michelle, Courtney, and Tess.

Prom was being held in the ballroom at the hot new Hudson Hotel in Soho, but we'd rented a suite for the post-prom party. It also served as a depot for all our prom essentials, such as a change of clothes and breath spray.

Mackenzie had brought Bennett. She figured, why not? He was hot and would look good in pictures.

Michelle was there with Henry Oregon. Sure, he had a high GPA, but he clearly wasn't that smart because she'd also easily convinced him to be her date.

It had only taken one pushed thought.

Tess was there with Teddy. As friends. Dave was with Lindsay. Daniel was with Rayna. After the twins lost their ESP, Rayna decided she liked the other twin better. Teddy was still hoping to get in on that. Sadie was here with Dumbo's roommate. We called him Dumbo II, even though his ears were perfectly normal. Mars was there with Mona, who was feeling much happier now that he was out of her head.

Pi was there with Jon.

Courtney was there with Jordana. Which was useful because when she realized she'd forgotten her makeup upstairs, she turned to Jordana and commanded, *Go up to the suite and get my lip gloss.* She needed to look her best when they announced the royal couple. It would be her for sure. She'd done a little bit of pushing but, come on, did she even have to bother? She was obviously going to win. She was a star.

Cooper was there with Olivia. Like he was supposed to be. Mackenzie belonged to the past. He belonged with Olivia. It was time to dance. He loved to dance. He was a good dancer.

The music slowed and he pulled her close to him. Yes. Everything was going to be fine. He would move into the dorms. He would date Olivia. He would go to NYU. He would smoke a little pot. He would even play a little poker, now that he was telepathy-free. Why not? Life could be easy again.

He saw Mackenzie dancing with Bennett across the room.

He looked away.

Mackenzie wasn't good for him. Yes, he'd loved her. But it had hurt too much. Maybe it was better to be with someone who loved you more than you loved her.

Michelle, who was standing nearby with Henry, felt her heart hurt for Olivia. No one wanted to be second best.

It almost made her want to give Olivia the crown.

Almost, but not quite.

Anyway, it was too late.

Suddenly, everyone stopped moving as Principal Roth, holding two large envelopes and wearing sunglasses, announced it was time for the coronation.

BJ was at the bar spiking his Coke when the principal called out his name.

"Wahoooo!" everyone yelled, going wild.

He hadn't been expecting that. Back when he'd started high school, everyone had just thought of him as a pervert. But maybe being with Tess had made him more loveable? Feeling a little tipsy, he pushed his way to the podium.

Tess's heart swelled when she heard his name. *Maybe it will give him his mojo back?*

Principal Roth tore open the second envelope, and we all held our breath. "And the winner is…" He looked around for effect. "Michelle Barak!"

"Yes!" screamed Michelle. "Yes! Yes! Yes!"

Michelle pushed her way forwards and grabbed her crown. She had done it! Long live the queen!

"What?" yelled Courtney. "Are you kidding me? I want a recount!"

The rest of us cheered. Our powers might have been disappearing, but at the very least, we had made a queen.

Just before the crowning, having zero interest in high school royalty, Pi and Jon had escaped to the roof.

Also, she didn't want to be photographed. Who knew how that would affect her position at Diamond – if she'd still have a position, that is.

Tick tock, tick tock. We were dropping like flies. Pi was hoping to see the moon but, unfortunately, the sky was covered with clouds. A cool wind was blowing, and in the distance they could hear the rumble of thunder. A storm was coming.

Suddenly, the deck lit up a brilliant white color and a large crack echoed. The wind picked up with a frightening roar and, fifteen storeys below, trees began to bend. They started running back inside, and ducked into the building and into the elevator, seconds before the rain came crashing down.

But they were going nowhere. The moment the elevator doors closed, everything went dark.

"You okay?" Jon asked.

"Of course I'm okay. Why wouldn't I be okay?"

He fumbled for his phone, and turned it on. In the dim light, he was able to locate the elevator's alarm and emergency phone, but nothing was working. So he tried calling on his cell, but couldn't get a signal.

"The outage must be widespread," he said matter-of-factly. "Cell towers have backup systems, but networks can become congested during blackouts."

"Thank you, Captain Obvious," she said, "but what do we do now?" Talk about awkward. They were trapped in an elevator. Together. Crammed in a tiny space. And who knew for how long?

"We can try the escape hatch," he said.

"And what happens if the power comes on while we're in the middle of climbing? We'll be chopped in half."

He shrugged. "I guess we'll just have to wait it out." *If this is citywide, we could be here for hours.*

"That's your suggestion? Wait it out?"

"I have Angry Birds," he said. "We can knock out some pigs."

"Don't you think we should save the battery? Just in case we're stuck here for hours?"

"Good point. I have another idea," he said, smiling coyly. *I'm going to kiss you.*

"Don't even think about it," she said, her cheeks heating up.

"Why not? Do you like me or not?"

"I do like you," she said. "But I like to be in charge." She moved in. "So I'm going to kiss *you.*"

It started lightly, his lips as soft as a feather.

Then he pulled her closer, his mouth pressing down on hers. She closed her eyes and, for one moment, let everything go.

He pulled back. "I knew you were my type."

"Shut up and kiss me again."

"Whatever you say, honey Pi."

"I told you not to call me that. If you think—" She stopped in mid-sentence.

"What is it?" he asked.

Must find alarm, she heard. *Emergency lighting... What if someone sees?* "There's someone out there," she said.

"I didn't hear—"

"Shh! I'm trying to listen."

It suddenly dawned on her that she could hear through the walls. The magnesium must have just kicked in. Yes! Finally! But it was hard work. Thoughts were coming to her in random pulses and she could barely make them out. "I think it's

Jordana," she said, after a few moments. "Jordana!" she yelled, while pounding on the doors. "Can you hear me? We're stuck in the elevator!"

"What's happening?" Jon asked. "Can you see what she's doing?"

"Do I look like I'm an X-ray machine? Wait. She's thinking something about a fire. A fire in the hotel. There's a fire and we're stuck in an elevator! Jordana, call someone!"

She heard nothing.

"Damn. She can't hear me. She must be in one of her trances."

"Stay calm," Jon said. "We're just have to—"

"Quiet! I'm trying to concentrate!" Pi stood perfectly still, staring ahead at the elevator doors. "There's no fire," she said finally. "Except…she's thinking about pulling the fire alarm. Why is she pulling the fire alarm if there's no fire?"

The alarm sounded, flooding the elevator with its pulsating clangs.

It occurred to her that if the magnesium was working, the cognizin citicoline should be working, too. She could probably push a command to Jordana, providing, of course, she could break through the first trance. Maybe it depended on the stronger command.

JORDANA! she mentally screamed as loud as she could. *GET HELP IMMEDIATELY! WE'RE STUCK IN THE ELEVATOR!*

She strained to hear a response, but all she got was static. And a massive headache.

"Oh, no," she said, and turned to Jon. "No, no, no!"

"What is it?" he asked.

"Think something!"

"Why?"

"Just do it!"

He stood there, staring.

And then, just like that, her headache was gone.

And so was her ESP.

"I can't hear a thing," she said in a dull voice.

"Maybe she went downstairs," he suggested.

"I'm talking about my ESP," she said tightly. "It's gone."

And so was Diamond.

She plopped down on the elevator floor, feeling the weight of defeat.

"Is it really so bad?" he asked gently.

"Seriously? I've just lost everything, and you're asking me if it's really so bad?"

"You don't need it, Pi. You're a genius all on your own."

"Yeah, well, what do you know?" she said, her eyes starting to sting. She could not cry. No way. She could not cry in front of Jon Matthews. She would not let herself lose control. "I don't get it. I finally get enhanced, and then I lose everything. That hardly seems fair."

"Shit happens," he said, and sat down next to her.

"Indeed. Shit happens and then you die," she said morosely.

"Or maybe, shit happens and then you move forwards?" he asked.

"How?" she asked.

"There's still Harvard," he said. "You'll have to apply again next year. But I have no doubt they'll accept you."

"There's that," she said. Of course they'd accept her. She had a killer GPA and now she had a killer essay topic.

What it's like to lose ESP.

In an elevator.

At prom.

She could do it if she put her mind to it. She would get through this, and she would succeed.

She always did.

"Hey, these shoes are expensive! Watch it, asshole!"

Downstairs in the ballroom, even with the emergency lighting, everyone was bumping into each other and tripping all over the place. But we all turned on the flashlight on our phones, and the place lit up like Christmas. Since there was no power for a mic, Principal Roth was at the podium, screaming at the top of his lungs. "Keep calm! The fire department is on its way! We have to evacuate the building! Follow me!"

Seriously? It was pouring outside. Rain might be just the ticket for a fire, but it was disastrous if you'd just come from the priciest salon in Soho. *Will my extensions fall out? ... My makeup is going to run down my face! ... Can we get a refund? This tux is a rental! ... The rain turns me on ... I really need to pick a wedgie.*

We followed Principal Roth out through a hallway, into the alley behind the hotel. There was a large overhead awning, and we all scrambled to fit underneath. It wasn't that bad, actually. Five or six flasks had materialized out of nowhere, and we began to warm up. After a few minutes, the rain slowed to a drizzle, and we practically tumbled into the alley. "Wassa a rittle lain?" one guy asked, stumbling on his feet. "Time to parteee!" One of the limo drivers flooded the alley with the brights of his car, and two other drivers were now doing the same. One connected his phone to his supercharged speaker, and a lot of us were dancing.

Best prom ever?

Teddy, who was now totally wasted, grabbed hold of Tess and twirled her around. BJ, who was there on his own, saw this and sprinted over. "Stop sleazing all over my girlfriend, Barboza!"

He grabbed Teddy's arm and yanked him away.

"Hey!" Teddy called out. Then he performed the same wrestling move that he had performed on Alan.

BJ landed on the ground with a thud.

Tess screamed.

"I'm okay," BJ said. "It's just my pride that's bruised. And maybe my ass."

Tess knelt down. "What were you doing?"

"I don't know," he said. "I'm a lover, not a fighter."

She laughed. "There is nothing going on between me and Teddy! We're just friends!"

"But how do *I* know that if I can't hear you?"

"Because I love *you*, you moron! I love you! You know that, don't you? It's you. It's only you."

I love you, too, he thought. *I'm sorry for being an idiot. I don't care if you read my mind. Go into my head whenever you want.*

Feed off my thoughts. Or feed off my body. Either is good.

She planted a wet kiss on his lips.

Oh, and from now on you have to call me Your Majesty, BJ thought. *Just in bed, though.*

BJ was thinking a lot of other things too, but it was all muffled in Tess's head. Something about a naked curtsey. She knew her ESP was going, but she didn't care. She knew he loved her. Or rather, she felt it.

On the other side of the makeshift outdoor dance floor, Cooper was dancing with Olivia. He liked to dance. He liked Olivia. The mist from the rain felt great on his face.

He was high.

Then he saw Mackenzie on the other side of the street. Crying.

He didn't mean to ditch Olivia. Didn't mean to leave her standing there by herself. He saw Mackenzie crying and just reacted.

Olivia was in mid-move when he walked away. *Well, that was embarrassing,* she thought.

Then she saw his arms around Mackenzie.

Her chest tightened. Her mind started to race. *No,* she told herself. *Stop.*

And she did. Instead, she turned around and kept dancing.

It was then that Jordana stumbled into the alley, looking confused.

"I've been looking for you everywhere," Courtney said. "Where have you been? You've been gone for ever! I lost the vote. Can you believe it? Did you at least remember my lip gloss?"

"Lip gloss?" Jordana repeated. "You want your lip gloss?"

"You didn't get it?" *Go back and get my lip gloss this instant! And, while you're there, get me some aspirin. My head is killing me!*

But Jordana didn't budge. "You look upset," she said. "Is there something on your mind?"

"What is the matter with you? Get me my lip gloss and some aspirin!"

"Get it yourself," Jordana retorted, and walked away.

Courtney's ESP was gone, along with her assistant.

On the other side of the street, Cooper put his hand on Mackenzie's shoulder. "Are you going to tell me what's wrong?" he asked. "If Bennett hurt you, I'll kill him."

"Those were happy tears, not sad tears. My mom called. She *called* me, Cooper. She can talk." Fresh tears dampened her face.

"Hey," he said, and hugged her. "That's amazing! Hurrah! We should celebrate!"

She looked at his red eyes. "It looks like you already celebrated."

"Just a little."

"Cooper…"

"What?"

"You need to get it together."

"I am! I am totally together. What about you? Where's your boy toy?"

She motioned with her chin. He had his arm around

Jordana. "He found a bigger, brighter Espie."

"Ah. Sorry."

She raised an eyebrow.

"Fine, I'm not sorry he's gone. But I am sorry you got ditched."

"Well, don't be. We were using each other anyway."

He shook his head. "I don't want to know."

She blushed. She looked out at the awning, and then back at him.

He still had his arms around her.

She looked over at Olivia. Her back was turned to them. She was probably pissed. Rightly so. "I'm gonna go."

"You're leaving? Now? At least stay for one dance. One last dance with me."

She shook her head. "I can't, Cooper."

"Why not? What's a little rain?" He was joking, but it was just a facade. He didn't want her to go. Something felt unfinished, something left unsaid. "Don't go," he said softly, brushing back a lock of her hair. "I don't want you to."

"I need to see my mom," she said. "Go back to Olivia, Cooper. She loves you."

"I know," he said, looking into her eyes.

Go, she commanded him. She knew her enhancement had kicked in.

Then she turned around and walked away.

It was the least she could do.

As she walked away her head started to burn.

One push, and her ESP was done.

Maybe Nick was right. You had it for as long as you needed, and then it was gone.

At first, Olivia wouldn't even look at him.

"Why are you mad at me?" Cooper asked.

"I turned around and you were hugging Mackenzie," Olivia said.

"I kissed her," he blurted, and she froze. He hadn't planned on saying that. It had just come out.

"What did you say?"

He drew in a breath. He had to come clean.

"I kissed her. On the cruise. You and I were fighting, and she was out on the deck."

"Mackenzie," she said matter-of-factly. "I can't say I'm surprised. And now you're breaking up with me."

"No. No! I'm being honest, Liv. It was a mistake. But I don't want to keep secrets. Not anymore. I want us to have a fresh start. I've been an ass, and I want to try again."

She shook her head, eyes wide. "Are you kidding me? No."

"Come on, Liv," he said, taking her arm. "I told you, it was a mistake."

She brushed his hand away. "This isn't about that. I mean, it is, but it's more than that. I can't do this anymore. I can't be with you. I was going to stay here to be with you. I would have done anything for you. And you…you never really cared about me at all."

"That's not true! You're amazing. And I want to be with you."

"I'm sorry," she said. "But I don't want to be with you."

"Come on, Liv," he said, sounding desperate. "Don't do this. What about school? We have a plan."

"What's the plan? I follow you to the one school you applied to because you were, what, too lazy to apply to any others?"

"I'm not lazy. I just…don't know what I want."

"I think you need to figure it out," Olivia said.

He half-smiled. "So now you're a therapist?"

"I'm sorry, Cooper. I care about you. I always will. And I hope we can stay friends. But you're not in love with me. And I don't like who I am when I'm with you."

His whole face crumpled. "So I'm Archer, then. You know, that dude in the book you liked. He ends up alone, too."

"*The Age of Innocence,*" she said. "Right. Except it was Mackenzie who liked that book, not me." She gave him a sad smile. "I'll see you around, Cooper."

He watched her walk away.

Principal Roth was yelling something from under the awning, so we all crowded in to hear. He gave the all-clear notice, and everyone cheered. The firemen had made a thorough sweep of the hotel and had found nothing suspicious, not even a smoldering ashtray. So even though the alley was fun in a campy sort of way, we were all cold and wet and went back inside. All of us except Mackenzie, who'd gone home to see her mom.

The power came on as we were spilling out of the stairwell onto the third floor. The hallway lit up like a stadium and the elevator opened with a ding, revealing Pi and Jon fumbling with their clothes.

"That is amazing," Levi said. "Go, honey Pi!"

Michelle covered her eyes. "Ow! I can't look!"

But it wasn't seeing Pi and Jon in a compromising position that was making her close her eyes. Her head hurt.

She was the last one to lose it, and the end was sharp and swift.

Henry put his arm around her. "You okay? Can I get you a glass of water?"

She might have lost her ESP, but at least she'd found her prince.

Chapter Twenty-Nine
"I"

Even though the hotel cameras had been on battery backup, the footage was way too fuzzy to make an ID. Which was a lucky break for Jordana, seeing how setting off prank fire alarms is a criminal offense. Not that she did it deliberately. And since she didn't remember any of it, the questions remained, who pushed her and why? Because someone must have pushed her. This was Jordana. She never would have figured out how to do it on her own.

Naturally, everyone thought of Courtney. Courtney made her do stuff all the time. Plus she'd been furious about losing. Courtney, of course, was indignant. She might be vain and petty, but she wasn't evil. All she wanted was her lip gloss, not to ruin prom.

That Sunday in the hotel suite, the Espies who'd stayed over discussed this ad nauseam. It was also the last Espie meeting they ever had.

At first they figured, *Why keep meeting?* Their ESP was gone.

The truth was, they needed space apart.

Except for Tess and BJ – no surprise there.

By the time Tess and BJ got to Berkeley, they had decided to move in together. Without their ESP, they were even closer.

"Sometimes," Tess said, "you have to ignore the mind and let the heart rule."

Excuse me while I go and throw up.

Yes.

I said it. *I.*

Who am I, you ask? You mean you don't know? Who do you think got Jordana to set off the alarm? Come on, admit it. They deserved it. When they weren't interrupting me or flat-out ignoring me, they were making fun of me. What's wrong with the way I dress? And what did they have against fencing?

But I got the best revenge. They all lost their ESP and, here it is, seven months later, and I'm still going strong.

I bet you're wondering where they all are today, now that they're just average. Like Tess and BJ, most of them went off to college. Even though the news leaked that they were no longer telepathic, none of the colleges reneged. Which was a good thing for the Espies with lower GPAs. They had to take their final exams and, let me tell you, it wasn't pretty.

But some of them took another route. Like the twins, for example. They went to Vegas just as they'd planned, only now they're selling timeshares. Courtney is doing another reality show, only this one's called *I Was a Teenage Psychic*. She does the same thing she did on her other show – absolutely nothing. Jordana's in beauty school. She's planning to open a nail salon as soon as her parents lend her the money.

Cooper enlisted in the army. In July, he was walking along Chambers Street when he spotted Jarred, one of the guys he'd played poker with in Jersey. Jarred saw Cooper and saluted, then went into the recruitment center. Cooper followed. If anything could help Cooper get his shit together, the army could.

After ten weeks of boot camp at the post in Missouri, he was shipped out to Arizona, where he gets to use his gaming skills while learning to fly drones.

He's happy.

He's now on leave for Christmas. At the moment, he's thinking about how peaceful it is as he strolls through Battery Park. He's remembering the time he brought Mackenzie flowers. When she was wearing the yellow dress.

From his thoughts, I can tell that he's noticed a girl in a green bomber jacket and a fuzzy woolen hat. She's sitting on a bench, staring ahead.

He thinks about that book from school, but he can't remember the title. It's something about innocence, and of a time long ago. Wasn't there a scene where the girl doesn't realize that the guy is watching her, and she doesn't turn around? But what if it ended differently? What if she sensed him standing there on the shore, then turned around and smiled?

It was Mackenzie's favorite book, even though it made her sad. She had to read it again this fall, at Stanford. She's double majoring in English lit and design. She loves it.

He decides to move in closer and realizes that it's her. Mackenzie. On the bench. On *their* bench. She's home for the holidays, too.

We can't go back, he thinks, *but we can go forward.* He knows he loves her. He's always loved her. She's what he's been missing. *Mackenzie, please, if you'd just turn around...*

She's thinking about him, too. About how different he looked in that picture he'd posted after he enlisted. He looked taller, somehow. More confident. Stronger, too.

I can't get him out of my mind...

If she turns around...

It's like he's here...

Boo-ya! Yes! She's turning around!

As for Olivia, she's at the top of her class at NYU, and is dating a psych major who is just as crazy about her as she is about him.

And, of course, let's not forget Pi. She decided to spend the year backpacking with Jon. She reapplied to Harvard for next year and feels pretty confident that she'll get in. She's cocky like that.

Here's a riddle for you: what do bananas and fertilizer have in common? If you guessed potassium, ding! But who knew it would save my ESP? At least, I'm pretty sure that's what did it. I binged on bananas like they were potato chips, and now here I am at Diamond.

I have to admit, though, Pi's experiment was brilliant. If it hadn't been for those supplements, I wouldn't be who I am today.

The most powerful person in the world.

Seriously, these enhancements are amazing. Especially when you triple the dosage. Consequences? Hah! The only consequence is that I'm the ultimate spy-machine. I can hear your every thought, no matter where you are.

New York. San Francisco. Australia.

Relax. I'm not a monster. I'm not evil. I can even be fun, when the mood hits. Take this push thing, for instance. Mix it with long distance, and it really gets interesting. How do you think Mackenzie got the idea to turn around? I mean, it's not like she could hear Cooper thinking. In order to do that relay thing, I'd actually have to be there.

Wouldn't I?

Wrap your head around that.

Before I go, I'll offer you a word of advice. If you're thinking of cheating on a test, or a boyfriend or girlfriend, if I were you, I'd think twice.

Someone might be listening.

Acknowledgments

Thank you to Laura Dail, Tamar Rydzinski, Deb Shapiro, Lauren Walters, Katie Hartman, Chloe Ashford, Veronique Baxter, Laura West, Nikole Eriksen and Wendy Loggia.

Everyone at Orchard: Jessica Tarrant, Belinda Jones and Thy Bui.

Thank you to all my friends, family, supporters and writing buddies including:

Targia Alphonse, Elissa Ambrose, Robert Ambrose, Jess Braun, Jeremy Cammy, Avery Carmichael, Ally Carter, the Dalven-Swidlers, James Eyler, the Finkelstein-Mitchells, Adele Griffin, Emily Jenkins, Lauren Kisilevsky, Aviva Mlynowski, Larry Mlynowski, Lauren Myracle, Jess Rothenberg, Courtney Sheinmel, Jennifer E. Smith, the Swidlers, Robin Wasserman and Louisa Weiss.

The loves of my life: Todd, Chloe and Anabelle.

One year + one beach house + zero parents =

TEN THINGS WE SHOULDN'T HAVE DONE

Read on for a taster of what happens when April is left home alone in Sarah Mlynowski's hilarious summer read!

Saturday, March 28th
THE MORNING AFTER

I bolted awake. A police siren.

The police were outside my house. Ready to arrest me for underage partying, excessive flirting, and an overcrowded hot tub.

But wait.

Brain turned on. No, not the cops. Just my phone – my dad's ringtone.

Which was even worse.

I rummaged around the futon. No phone. Instead I felt a leg. A guy's leg. A guy's leg flung over my ankle. A guy's leg that did not belong to my boyfriend.

Oh God. Oh God. What have I done?

WEEEooooWEEEooooWEEEoooo!

Upstairs. The siren ring was coming from upstairs, the main level of Vi's house.

Maybe if I closed my eyes, just for a teeny-tiny second... No! Phone ringing. In bed with not my boyfriend. I managed to get myself out of the futon without disturbing him and – um, where were my trousers? Why was I in bed with a guy who was not my boyfriend without my trousers on?

At least I had underwear on. And a long-sleeved shirt. I looked around for some trousers. The sole item of clothing within grabbing distance was Vi's red dress that I wore last night for the party.

That dress was trouble.

I ran up the stairs bare-legged. At the top, I almost passed out.

It looked like a war zone. Empty plastic cups littered the wooden floor. Half-eaten tortilla chips were planted in the shag carpet like pins on a notice board. A large blob – punch? Beer? Something I'd be better off not identifying? – had stained the bottom half of the pale blue curtain. A white lace bra hung from the four-foot cactus.

Brett was in surfer shorts, face-down on the sofa. He was using the purple linen tablecloth as a blanket. Zachary was asleep in one of the dining room chairs, wearing an aluminum foil tiara on his lolled-back head. The patio door was open – and a puddle of rain had flooded the carpet.

WEEEooooWEEEooooWEEEoooo! Phone was louder. Closer. But where? The kitchen counter? The kitchen counter! Nestled between a saucer of cigarette butts and an empty bottle of schnapps! I dived towards it. "Hello?"

"Happy birthday, Princess," my dad said. "Did I wake you?"

"Wake me?" I asked, my heart thumping. "Of course not. It's

already" – I spotted the microwave clock across the room – "nine thirty-two."

"Good, because Penny and I are almost there."

"Almost in New York?" I asked.

"Almost in Westport. Almost at your place!"

Terror seized me. "What does that mean?"

My dad laughed. "We decided to surprise you on your birthday. It was actually Penny's idea."

"Wait. Really?"

"Of course! Surprise!"

My head was spinning, and I felt like vomiting and it wasn't just because of the many, many, definitely too many glasses of spiked punch I had consumed last night. My father could not see this place. No, no, no.

Oh God. I'd violated 110 per cent of my dad's rules. The evidence was all around, mocking me.

This wasn't happening. It couldn't happen. I would lose everything. If, after last night, I had anything left to lose. I took a step and a tortilla chip attacked my bare foot. *Owww*.

Mother friggin' crap.

"That's great, Dad," I forced myself to say. "So…you're at LaGuardia?"

It would take them at least an hour to drive here from the airport. Could I make this house look presentable in an hour? I would find some trousers. Then I would toss the bottles and cups and cigarette butts and vacuum the tortilla chips and maybe the bra, maybe even Brett and Zachary—

"Nope, we just drove through Greenwich. We should be

there in twenty minutes."

Twenty minutes?!

There was groaning from the sofa. Brett flipped onto his back and said, "It's eff-ing freezing in here."

"April, there's not a boy staying, is there?" my dad asked.

I sliced my hand through the air to tell Brett to shut the hell up.

"What? No! Of course not! Vi's mom is listening to NPR."

"We just passed the Rock Ridge Country Club. Looks like we're making better time than I thought. We'll be there in fifteen minutes. Can't wait to see you, Princess."

"You too," I choked, and hung up. I closed my eyes. Then opened them.

Two half-naked boys in the great room. One in a tiara.

More half-naked boys in the bedrooms.

A hundred empty bottles of booze.

And Vi's mom nowhere in sight.

I was a dead princess.

April and her best friend, Vi, are living by themselves. Of course, April's parents don't know that. It's a little white lie that begins the ten things April and Vi shouldn't have done – things that definitely make their lives a LOT more interesting!

*From **Skipping School** (#3) and **Throwing a Crazy Party** (#8) to **Buying a Hot Tub** (#4) and, um, **Harbouring a Fugitive** (#7), April's story is hilarious, bittersweet – and not for the faint-hearted...*

Don't miss
Ten Things We Shouldn't Have Done –
OUT NOW!

PB: 9781408309797 • Ebook: 9781408313763

Two friends. Five countries.
And one boy who's cute in any language...

DON'T MISS

THE GiRL'S GUIDE TO SUMMER

COMING 2017

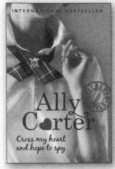

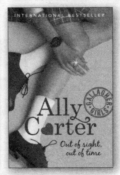